HAVING THE DEMON'S BABY

CHAOTIC CONCEPTIONS SERIES

BOOK THREE

COURTNEY DAVIS

Published by:

5 Prince Publishing and Books, LLC

DBA 5 Prince Publishing

PO Box 865

Arvada, Colorado 80001

Digital ISBN: 978-1-63112-439-6

Print ISBN: 978-1-63112-440-2

Cover design by Marianne Nowicki

Interior design by 5 Prince Publishing

First Edition F042826

For more information about this title, visit: www.5princebooks.com

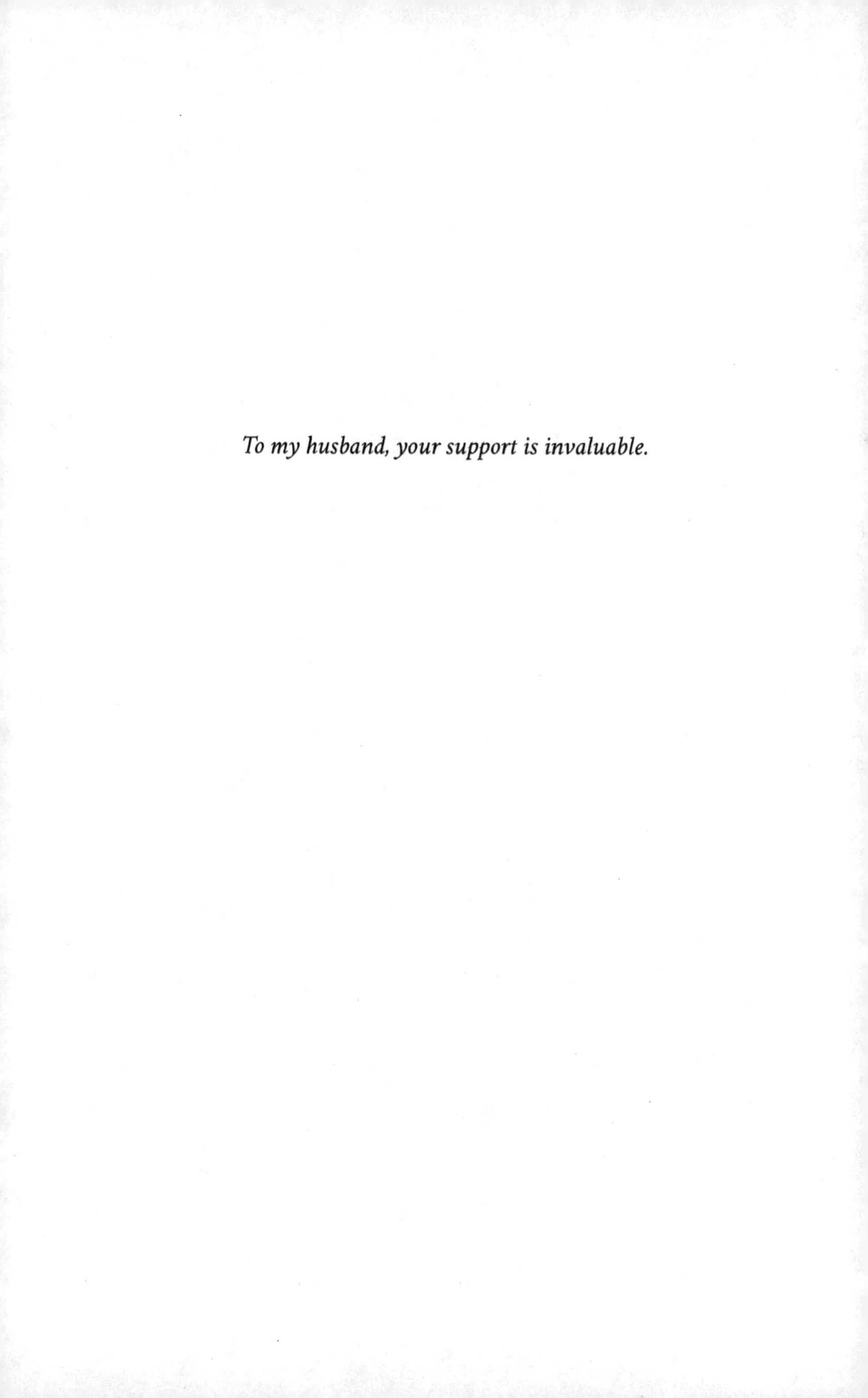

To my husband, your support is invaluable.

ACKNOWLEDGMENTS

Thank you, Bernadette, for believing in my writing journey.

And thank you, Cate, for helping me turn my drafts into something I can be proud of.

ALSO BY COURTNEY DAVIS

Chaotic Conception Series

Having the Vampire's Baby

Having the Werewolf's Baby

Having the Demon's Baby

The Atlantis Series

The Vampires of Atlantis

Aristotle's Wolves

Descendants of Atlantis

Stand Alone Titles

Butterfly Kisses

The Serpent and the Firefly

A Spider in the Garden

Princess of Prias

Soul Sacrifice

A Shadow Among the Stars

Demons and Tea Leaves

Trusting the Alpha

HAVING THE DEMON'S BABY

PROLOGUE

Levi Blackwood sat behind his desk and stared at the retreating woman with a glower. He hit the button to unmute the video call as soon as the door shut, blocking her from his view.

"Leviathan, are you insane? You hired her?" The voice of his brother grated Levi's ears after the honeyed tones he'd been getting from Angelica Walsh.

Levi knew what Foras was suggesting. "Why wouldn't I? Her resume is exquisite."

"So is her ass, I'm guessing, by the way your eyes flared as she walked away," Foras snickered.

Levi glared at his brother on the screen and hit the *end call* button. He had no idea why his younger brother enjoyed listening to him interview potential secretaries. It was usually the most mundane part of Levi's day, and it happened all too often since most of them only lasted a month or two.

He doubted Angelica, who had told him at least twice to call her Angie but never Ms. Walsh, would last any longer than the others. On the surface it was an easy job—take calls and fetch coffee—but as soon as they found out he was a demon they tended to get skittish. Then he started to get pissed, which made them more skittish, and they soon quit. As if he didn't have enough problems running the largest construction firm in Larkspring, he had to constantly hire secretaries.

He picked up her resume and read through it again. Angelica was more than qualified for the position. Most recently she'd been a secretary up in San Francisco for a banker, a position she'd held for three years. She was looking for a job now because she'd gotten a divorce and just moved here.

There was no reason not to hire her. After a week of filling in, Sharon was getting run ragged. He wasn't fond of the half demon being his secretary as well as the front desk receptionist for the entire floor. It was a busy company and the two positions were full time. He needed someone dedicated to his needs alone. The problem was, not many were applying anymore and Angelica was also exactly the type he usually sought for his personal needs. He tended to avoid secretaries that attracted him, or were demons, because spending too much time with a demon female could insinuate things even if it was a working relationship.

Angelica didn't fall into the demon category, however, she looked as though she'd only come up to his chest without those high heels she'd had on, and she was curvy in a way that made him think about putting his hands all over her. Her red hair was wild and curled around as if it refused to be tamed and she had caramel eyes that popped out of her pale and freckled face. The combination made her seem innocent, and boy did that make him want to corrupt her.

His dick hardened and he knew he had made a mistake in hiring her instead of hitting on her. Even a demon knew you shouldn't fuck where you work. It was going to be torture to see her at the desk outside of his office for however long she was there. The one saving grace was that he knew she'd only be there for a short time.

CHAPTER 1

One Year Later

Angie wasn't sure how she'd managed to work for that asshole for an entire year. Apparently no one else could believe it either, because they were throwing her a one-year anniversary party. They'd also thrown her a six-month anniversary party since that had been a shocking achievement on its own.

She agreed that she deserved it.

In the beginning it had seemed like every time she figured out how to anticipate one of Levi's needs he switched them around just so he could glare at her. Which was something he did constantly no matter if she'd supposedly messed anything up or not. She had learned a few tricks in those first months that smoothed things out, like making sure he had ice on Fridays or after an important meeting because that's when he wanted his whiskey. He didn't say thank you, but he was less irritable.

His terrible attitude didn't take away from his wickedly good looks. He was every bit the demon dreamboat that she'd heard about when looking into the job. He had black hair and eyes, flawless olive-toned skin, and dramatic eyebrows. His jaw was square and his lips were plump when he wasn't smashing them into an angry thin line. The few times she'd seen his teeth in a sneer, they were straight and white. His body, which was always draped perfectly in an expensive suit, was tall and even under the fabric she could tell he was toned.

She knew he worked out daily, his schedule was as familiar to her as her own, since she was the one who added most things to it. He went to the gym to lift weights on a lower floor five days a week and swam in the gym pool the other two. He was everything she normally drooled over. To be fair she did drool over him, too, on occasion. She would never do anything about it, demons intimidated her in the dating realm.

There were rumors that they could breathe fire, she doubted that, and that they could shapeshift and blend with the night. None of that had been substantiated beyond rumors however, and she'd never seen anything to indicate anything like that in the year she'd worked for him. What she had seen was he had a temper and he liked things his way, but that wasn't unusual for a man with as much money and influence as he had. So despite the fact that she often dreamed of him in various erotic scenarios, she was glad he'd never tried to cross any lines with her. He was also so frustrating most days that she couldn't get over it enough to appreciate his good looks.

Her desperation to keep the job was the only reason she was standing in the breakroom of the office after a year while champagne and cake was passed around after hours.

"I don't know how you did it and we are all thankful," Sharon said as she refilled Angie's flute for the third, or was it the fourth, time. Angie didn't care, she was enjoying herself because the booze was free and she had a bonus on the way.

"I am a very detail-oriented type," Angie said. "I pay attention to what he likes." And when he changes what he likes, she rolls with it.

"I never thought he'd keep someone around that he wasn't interested in," Sharon said. "Maybe because you're human it doesn't count."

Angie wasn't sure what Sharon meant by that statement but she shrugged it off. Sharon had worked at the company for as long as it had been open and had seen all the secretaries come and go for Levi. When there was a lapse, she had to do the job. Sharon was a tall and robust woman with a motherly vibe who dressed in cardigan sweater sets and long skirts. She wore lots of beaded necklaces and kept her black hair short. She greeted everyone who came into the office as *hun,* even if she knew their name, and she never forgot anyone's birthday, anniversary, or start date. She was a huge reason that Angie had survived the first couple weeks. Every time she'd wanted to cry and run away she'd gone and talked to Sharon for a few minutes, and it would give her the strength to go back to her own desk. It just didn't make sense that Levi could be a terrible person and have hired on, and kept on, such a sweet person like Sharon. The fact that Sharon didn't seem intimidated by the man helped a lot too, it made Angie think he was all bluster and no bite, though she hadn't tested the theory herself.

"Cheers," Angie said and shot back half the glass, her head already starting to feel light.

"What are you going to do with the bonus?" Patrick asked, joining the conversation. Patrick was an accountant who'd been with the company for about six months. Young and optimistic, he was constantly telling Angie about his weekend party lifestyle. The man was fearless. Even though he was a human, he spent time in vampire bars and werewolf bars. He often recalled sexual encounters with the men who picked him up that made Angie's cheeks burn. Patrick was a short man with glasses and orange hair so he had the look of a quiet number cruncher, which made his escapades all the more surprising to her the first time he'd shared. Angie loved hearing his stories over sandwiches and salads in the breakroom every Monday. She lived vicariously through him, wishing she'd spent more of her twenties and early thirties being wild and less of it being in a disappointing marriage.

"Oh, I don't know," Angie hedged, even though she did know and it was a huge part of why she had applied for this job and why she'd put up with Levi for so long.

"You should go on a tropical vacation. You haven't used any of your vacation or sick days. Most of his secretaries called out sick on day two, some never returned," Sharon whispered as if the demon they worked for was listening.

She didn't know what Levi's abilities were exactly, but she was pretty sure that hearing rooms away wasn't one of them. In the last year she hadn't been able to add much to this list of traits beyond the famed demon anger and business sense. Sometimes it annoyed her that he was so private. She'd like to force his walls down, and his pants.

Oh shit, that was definitely the champagne talking, she usually stopped those thoughts before they fully formed in her brain.

"Yeah, maybe," she said, forcing herself back to the present, and the future. She held back the smile of excitement about what she was going to do. She was thirty-five, single, and about to get pregnant. She chugged the rest of the champagne in her glass and accepted another pour, maybe she would call in sick tomorrow.

An hour later Angie stumbled to her desk with alcohol-blurred vision, a stomach full of cake, and uncontrollable giggles. She was ecstatic because she'd just gotten the notification that her bonus was in her bank account. Now she was going to put her appointment in her calendar because nothing was real if it wasn't on the calendar.

8:00 am artificial insemination, Stonecroft Clinic

She hit the button that would enter it in and make it official. Then she slammed her laptop shut and stumbled to the elevator. Tomorrow morning she was going to take a huge step on her journey to being a parent. Doing it alone hadn't been her first choice, but she wasn't about to let a little thing like being single keep her from realizing her dream of motherhood.

Levi was sitting in his office when Angelica stumbled to her desk. Even with his door open she didn't seem to notice he was there, and he made no move to alert her. She was mussed in a way that made him jealous, even though he knew she hadn't just come from some rendezvous. He had given Sharon very strict orders to not only be sure everyone got home safe after the party, but under no circumstances to allow Angelica to have a drunken office fling. He didn't want to have to murder one of his employees. And that's what it would come to, because even though he hadn't ever declared himself in the demon tradition of courting, he was inexplicably drawn to possess her. If anyone else did, then it would mean he had lost, which was unacceptable.

Not that he ever planned to tell Angelica any of that, he planned to want her from afar until she quit and then he'd forget her. Courting and mating was not something he saw in his near future, and with her he knew there could be nothing less.

That didn't stop his mind from wandering, especially when she looked like she did tonight. Her red curls were falling out of the ponytail she'd restrained them in earlier and her black pencil skirt was slightly askew. She'd been wearing a black cardigan throughout the day which was missing now and allowed him to see how the purple satin sleeveless shirt clung to her. The sight of her large breasts pushing against the fabric that was unbuttoned one more than it had been all day, made his pants tighten. He wanted to run his tongue over her pale shoulders and he wanted to run his hand up her pantyhose-clad thighs.

He gripped the armrests of his chair and chastised himself for indulging in this nonsense. His nails lengthened and sharpened as if they were ready to cut the fabric right off of her body. It never did him any good to fantasize about her because he would never do anything about it. Not only did he instinctively know she wouldn't be just a fling for him, he also didn't want to be the type of boss who preyed upon his employees for sexual satisfaction. It was easy enough for him to find that elsewhere when he wanted it, which he hadn't in the last year. The problem was obvious, unattached demons didn't spend this much time in close proximity with someone they weren't interested in courting. And for the last year he had been forcing himself to ignore what he wanted. Which was no longer working very well seeing as he was so affected just by the sight of Angelica's shoulders, of all things. He really needed her to quit, it would be best for them both. She didn't react to him the way the other secretaries had. Or, as Sharon had pointed out after the first six months, maybe he didn't treat her quite as terribly as he'd treated the others. Honestly he thought he treated all of them the same, as if they should do whatever he needed them to do without being asked. It just seemed Angelica was the only one capable of actually living up to that standard. If she were a demon female he'd think it was a sign of their compatibility.

He watched her and willed his cock down as she headed back toward the elevators. He'd follow as soon as he heard the ding of the door closing, it was the same as every day since she'd started working for him.

He made it a point to never leave the office before her. A necessity since he'd seen her address written on her tax form that first day. It was just to be certain she was safe. He'd nearly demanded she move out of the only neighborhood of Larkspring he'd consider dangerous for a woman alone. There were no gangs in the city but there were drugs, and those who were under their influence more often than not. These people congregated where housing was cheap and police presence was low, and that's where Angelica had chosen to live. He'd followed her the first day to check things out and it became a habit he couldn't break. He always watched from a perch on a nearby roof, wings tucked close and his demon form blending with the night. He'd make sure she was safely inside, and then he paid a young vampire with nothing better to do to watch her apartment through the night until she was on her way back to his office.

On weekends Levi made it a point to know what she was up to and often had people nearby who kept an eye on her. A benefit of being a demon was that he always had other demons, mostly halflings, to call on to do things under the radar. He couldn't believe she'd never noticed, even though his people were very subtle. And they knew what kind of trouble they'd be in if they failed his orders to watch her and not be seen.

Levi got up from his desk and walked out of his office to follow her. His usual routine was to go up to his penthouse, sprout his wings on his balcony, then fly over to her neighborhood to wait for her. His phone chimed with an alert as he made his way to the elevators.

He stared at the calendar alert he'd just gotten with mouth agape. "She's getting herself pregnant?" he snarled.

The dam he'd built up over the last year that had been holding back all his possessive feelings and desire for Angelica, broke with that realization and his body flooded with angry heat, his demon form taking over. The smell of burning cotton and silk filled the lobby as his suit combusted. He grew a foot taller and sprouted his black leathery wings. His nails sharpened and elongated and his skin turned a deep maroon. He headed upstairs to his penthouse as the final shreds of singed and steaming fabric fell from him.

Levi owned the entire building and lived in a penthouse that encompassed most of the top floor. Thankfully, there was a private elevator that took him up. As he rode, he seethed, his wings flapping agitatedly and brushing against the walls. If Angelica got pregnant she would smell like some other man and he would have to find that man and kill him. Artificial insemination or not, he'd sniff out the father and eliminate the competition for claim over her. Because as much as he'd been denying it over the last year, that is exactly what he wanted, he wanted a claim over her that was undeniable and unbreakable.

If he did eliminate the competition, it wouldn't be the first time he intervened in her love life, though he'd never felt as if he needed to commit murder before. Of course the interventions he'd completed before were in large part to prevent things progressing to a point where he'd be faced with the desire for murder. Angie complained to Sharon about never being asked out on a second date since she moved to this city. She had no idea that it was because Levi threatened anyone she went out with and none had dared to risk his wrath for a second date.

He told himself it was Angelica's fault. If she'd just quit the job like everyone else then he wouldn't care what she did, because he wouldn't see her five days a week. Out of sight, out of mind. Having her running his life in this office made it impossible for him to stop thinking about her. A dark part of his soul liked to remind him that as soon as she'd walked into his office for an interview he'd lost a piece of himself to her. That no matter if she was in front of him every day or not, he'd never be able to stop thinking about her, desiring her and thinking that eventually, she'd be his.

He had ignored that voice and did what he could to get her to quit without giving her a reason to file a lawsuit against him. Somehow it hadn't worked and he was thankful every day that she'd continued to show up to his office.

A horrifying thought occurred to him as he rushed out of the elevator to his penthouse door. What if she quit after this? What if she'd only stuck it out this long so that she could make the bonus and pay for what he knew was a very expensive procedure?

It wasn't enough to stop her from being impregnated by someone else, he suddenly realized, he had to ensure she would never leave him. A grin spread across his face as the plan formed. There was one good way to ensure someone stayed in your life and she'd presented it to him on a calendar-updated platter.

CHAPTER 2

Drinking in your late thirties was no joke. Angie wanted to die when her alarm went off. She was up early because she had to get in and out of the fertility clinic before work, which meant there was no time for wallowing in self-induced misery. She pulled on a comfortable black dress and low heels then threw her hair up in a bun because it was at least one day past needing to be washed and she had no energy to do more. She skipped makeup, figuring she could put on a little in the bathroom at work when she was feeling less like she needed to constantly splash water on her face to stay alert.

The thought of what she was about to do overpowered her nausea and she managed to brush her teeth without gagging, then grabbed her purse. She turned the three locks on her apartment door and wrinkled her nose at the smell of stale cigarette smoke in the hallway. She lived in a dump, and she knew she was going to have to move before she had a baby. That was a problem for future her though, and she wouldn't even have it if she didn't get to the clinic. She locked her door and hurried down the hall then out the front door.

"Good morning Ms. Walsh."

Angie waved at the young vampire who was always stationed outside of her house in the morning. He didn't live in her building, but apparently he liked her shady stoop. "Morning Dalton." Vampires didn't need to avoid all sunshine, though some did, they just needed to be careful they didn't spend too much time in it. There had actually been great strides in the last year or two in developing some sunscreens that would extend their time without getting a burn. Dalton had a pale complexion so she didn't think he pushed his luck much.

"Woah, you don't look so great, are you sure you should be going to work today? And you're heading out about an hour earlier than usual."

"Are you my secretary, Dalton?" she laughed.

"Just know your schedule," he said with a shrug and ran a hand through his dyed blond locks. "Are you heading out for some cold medicine or something?" His gaze ran up and down her obvious work clothes and he frowned.

She'd gotten used to Dalton's apparent interest in her life and didn't find his questions odd anymore. She assumed he had a friend or girlfriend in the building that he waited for every morning. Whenever she asked him about it, he was vague with his answers, so maybe his girlfriend was married.

"I had too much celebration last night. I'll be fine after some coffee and breakfast," she explained.

"Oh, hangover. I thought people your age didn't do that sort of thing."

"We usually don't," she assured him as her cab pulled up. "See you tomorrow."

"What happened to your car?"

"Too much partying, remember. I got a ride home last night, I know better than to drink and drive."

"Smart chick."

She noticed him pull out what looked like a brand new phone as he stood and walked away from the stoop. She wondered how he could afford that and her heart hurt a little knowing whatever it was, it probably wasn't legal or sustainable. He seemed like a nice kid, maybe twenty with his whole life ahead of him. If she had the means to offer him help, she would.

Angie chugged water in the back of the cab and closed her eyes for the twenty-minute drive. She wasn't feeling any better when they stopped in front of the Stonecroft Clinic and she hoped they wouldn't turn her away. As soon as she stepped through the front doors a wave of healing washed over her. It shouldn't have been a surprise, this place was run by witches so it made sense that they spelled it to improve people's mood when they entered. This wasn't her first time in the clinic, but she'd never noticed it before, so maybe it only affected those who needed a boost.

They could make a fortune selling this spell, that was for sure. Instant hangover relief is something people would sell a lung for.

Angie walked to the front desk with a grin on her face and told the receptionist her name. "I'm here for insemination," she whispered excitedly.

"Congratulations, Ms. Walsh, I'm certain you'll be a mother in no time. If you'll have a seat, a nurse will call you back shortly. You're our first appointment of the day so it won't be long."

Angie could barely contain her excitement enough to sit, so she wandered around the empty waiting room. There were the typical parenting and home décor magazines on the tables for patients to read. The artwork on the walls was a step above hotel room with a decidedly maternal flair, nothing to hold her interest. She paced to the other side of the waiting area and noticed a framed photo she hadn't seen on any of her other visits. It was of the witch she'd been seeing for her fertilization, Felicity, and the vampire Senator Johnson Paulie. It was a staged publicity photo of them standing in front of the clinic shaking hands.

She knew the story behind that photo, this clinic had made it possible for Johnson's son to have a baby with a human. Angie shivered at the thought. She'd never even dated a guy that was another species, let alone considered having a kid with one. Her mind wandered without permission to her boss, her very sexy and very much a demon, boss. What would it be like to date a man like him? He was so controlling and so particular. He probably dictated everything that went on in the bedroom too.

Why did the idea of that intrigue her? It had to be the hangover, she was usually able to keep those sorts of thoughts at bay. Apparently excessive alcohol led to a wandering mind.

"Angelica Walsh," a nurse called out.

Angie hurried to the woman. "That's me."

"Hello Angelica, how are you feeling today? You look a little tired."

"I had a work celebration last night," she admitted.

"Ah, well, nothing wrong with that. You'll hopefully be missing out on those for a while if all goes as planned today."

"I hope so," she agreed.

The nurse led her to a room where she took Angie's blood pressure and temperature.

"Your vitals look good despite the late night. I'll let Felicity know you're ready. You just need to undress the bottom half and hop up on the table. It shouldn't be long."

Angie thought about the sperm she'd picked as she got herself ready. She'd gone for tall and handsome, well she assumed he was handsome, she hadn't seen a picture of the guy. His description said he was tall with dark hair and eyes, and olive skin. He was of Eastern European heritage and she thought it would mix well with her own Irish looks. His file said he worked out daily and he was college educated too, so that was a bonus. She wanted to give her child the best possible genetics to succeed in life. She ignored the realization that she'd picked someone who probably looked a lot like her boss. There was nothing behind that decision, just coincidence she assured herself.

"Good morning," Felicity said as she entered the room. "Are you ready for this big step?"

"I am," Angie said and felt tears prickle her eyes.

Felicity patted her hand as she looked over Angie's chart. "It looks like you are ready. It will just take a minute to get your sample. While you wait, I want you to meditate on what your life is going to be like with a bundle of joy added to it."

"I can definitely do that." Angie settled back and let her eyes close. She envisioned a nice apartment with lots of light to raise her child in. Something modern but also cozy with lots of color.

The door opened and the voice of the receptionist broke through Angelica's meditation.

"Sorry to interrupt, Felicity, but there's a ... man out there demanding to see you."

"Why—Oh, the goddess," the witch mumbled. "I will be back shortly and we'll finish this up."

Angie tried to go back to her meditation but her mind started to wander. She wondered what Mr. Blackwood was going to say when she told him she'd need maternity leave. Hopefully he wouldn't fire her, because she really needed the good health insurance his company provided. It was the second reason she'd chosen to work there despite his surly personality. He also had a great maternity leave policy so if she was careful, she'd be able to take twelve weeks off and get into a new apartment. If she was very careful.

Levi had walked into the Stonecroft Fertility Clinic and frowned at the feel of witch magic pushing at him and trying to make him calm. He didn't need to be calm, he needed to not be too late or he just might burn the whole place to the ground. He'd had to wait until Angelica was called back to a room before he walked in so she wouldn't see him and that made him nervous. How long did artificial insemination take?

"Can I help you with something?" the woman behind the front desk snapped at him.

He could tell immediately that she was a witch. It was something in their aura that he picked up on. It felt like no other creature he'd ever come across and it grated against his demon senses. He knew that she was getting a similar feeling from him, witches and demons didn't get along. He needed their help today though, so he forced himself to keep his temper and smooth his scowl.

He strode toward the woman. "I am Leviathan Blackwood and I need to speak with whoever is taking care of Angelica Walsh. Immediately."

"Is there some kind of emergency?"

"There will be if I don't get to speak with her doctor," he snarled, his carefully held control slipping and his skin heating.

She made an annoyed sound before she stood and walked through a door. She no doubt knew better than to challenge him. An older, more experienced witch, might not hesitate. But she seemed young, which might work in his favor. Time was of the essence.

Now he was waiting impatiently. There were two other people in the waiting room, both human women and they eyed him curiously. No doubt they thought he was there to sell his sperm. One looked like she was interested in what he might be leaving, the other looked terrified to even be in the same room as him, which usually meant she could tell what he was. Levi ignored them both and focused on the door he expected to open any moment.

He recognized Felicity Stonecroft when she walked into the waiting room from the picture on the website he'd checked out last night. She was a tall woman with long, blonde hair and bright, blue eyes. Her skin was flawless, typical of a witch, and her lips were painted a bright red. She had a simple green dress on under a lab coat and she gave off an air of authority. Her eyes widened when they landed on him and as she approached, her lips curled up in a smile that he wasn't expecting.

"The Moon Goddess approves of you, demon," she said in greeting.

"Sometimes," he agreed. They weren't always on good terms, however he could see that pointing this out to the witch wasn't likely to help his case. "You're doing Angelica Walsh's insemination today?"

"I would say that is confidential, but ..." she hesitated and her eyes went unfocused. "Ah, I see the goddess has her fingers in this one. Yes, I am about to do her insemination now. Why is that a concern of yours?"

"You are going to use my sperm."

She raised an eyebrow as if she were challenging his demand. "How do you know the woman?"

"Does it matter?" he growled.

"No," she said with a cackle. "Follow me."

Levi followed with a grunt, his skin cooling as his fear of missing his chance diminished. Felicity led him down a hallway to the door of a small, low-lit room. "I don't want her to know anything has changed from her plan."

"Because you don't want her to do anything about it before it's too late?" Felicity asked with curiosity, not judgment.

Levi lifted a corner of his upper lip and snarled, "Do we have an understanding?" He took the cup from her.

"You know I am a willing conduit of the goddess's mischief."

"So I've been told," he said darkly and walked into the room.

CHAPTER 3

"I'm sorry, it'll just be a few minutes. I'm waiting for the semen, it's being prepared right now," Felicity said when she came back into the exam room.

Angie didn't love lying on the paper-covered table, or delays in her schedule, but she'd do almost anything to have a baby. "I'm in a bit of a hurry, I didn't call out of work."

"Where do you work? I don't want you doing anything too strenuous today."

"I'm a secretary for Leviathan Blackwood over at Blackwood Construction."

"Of course you are," Felicity said with a smile. "Well, that shouldn't be a problem. I'll bet Mr. Blackwood will let you take it easy with his blessing."

Angie doubted it, but she didn't want to disagree with Felicity. If Levi complained about her being a few minutes late she'd work through her lunch or stay an extra couple of minutes at the end of the day. She pulled out her phone to see what was on the schedule for the day. If Levi didn't have an early appointment then he was less likely to be annoyed if she was late bringing him his coffee. She opened the calendar app where she had hers and

Levi's appointments showing together and color coded. Hers all showed up lilac, her favorite color, and his were gray like she imagined his morals to be. She needed to see both, but he only saw his own.

She stared at today's appointment and meetings list and felt her stomach turn. Right there highlighted in gray were the words: *8:00 am artificial insemination, Stonecroft Clinic*

She'd put it on *his* calendar. Panic filled her at the thought of him knowing what she was up to today. How early did he check his schedule? Usually he spent the morning at the gym and got into his office at about the same time as her. Her first duty of the day was to tell him about his appointments after she handed him his coffee. Did he ever check it at all?

She deleted the appointment and closed her eyes, sending up prayers to whoever might be listening that her boss didn't know what she was doing right now. The possible mortification was more than she could handle, she'd probably spontaneously combust if he knew.

"Here it is," Felicity announced when a nurse walked in looking irritated and holding a tray. A scent hit Angie that was familiar and completely out of place, but she quickly forgot it as she was instructed to lay back and put her feet in the stirrups.

Angie let all her worries go. It didn't matter. All that mattered was this moment and this amazing option. She had wanted a baby for so long and she was finally, probably, getting her wish.

"You're going to add extra magic, right? I know that my chances are low to get pregnant without help." She'd tried the old-fashioned way when she'd been married. They'd gone at it for two years before being told that she didn't have the most hospitable uterus and Grayson had a very low sperm count. When she'd suggested they use a sperm donor or a surrogate, he'd said he wasn't really sure he even wanted kids. They were divorced a year later and Angie began this journey of motherhood on her own. She'd taken a payout for half of the house they'd bought together, which hadn't amounted to much after lawyer fees and paying off the mortgage, then she'd packed her car and driven to Larkspring. She'd rented the first available apartment and accepted the first job offered that would meet her requirements.

And now she was here.

"All done," Felicity said, standing up between Angie's spread knees.

"That was fast."

"It's the easy part. Waiting the next few weeks before you can take a test to see if it worked isn't going to be."

Angie already knew waiting was going to be near impossible, so she had made plans to distract herself. She'd bought herself three new books and enough yarn to crochet two baby blankets. Admittedly the crocheting wasn't going to be a distraction so much as an indulgence and positive thinking, but it would keep her busy. She'd be working and living mostly as usual while hoping for the best result of this procedure.

Angie accepted Felicity's hand to sit up and felt a wetness between her thighs. "It's warm," she commented with a frown. "I thought the sperm was frozen."

"That's normal for this sort of thing," Felicity assured her. "How are you feeling?"

Angie did a quick self-assessment. She was feeling anxious and excited and still slightly hungover. "Good," she said with a smile.

"Take it easy the rest of the day. There's really nothing more you can do other than let your body and my magic create life."

"I will, thank you. I'm heading to work then home to sleep."

Felicity seemed satisfied with that answer. She gave Angie instructions for when to test and when to call her doctor. Then Angie was alone with the possibilities of motherhood and couldn't stop smiling as she got dressed.

. . .

Angie got to work exactly on time. Passing Sharon's desk, she waved quickly rather than stopping for her usual good morning exchange. Today Sharon was wearing a bright purple sweater set that her nails matched. When did she have time to do her nails? Yesterday they were blue, Angie was certain. Sharon was the first face people saw when they arrived to this floor, which held all the public offices for Blackwood Construction. Sharon was a warm juxtaposition to Levi's coldness and was likely the reason they got most of their business. She had the ability to put people at ease and Angie needed that right now.

"I want to chat later, is he already here?"

"Nope, you may have beaten him by thirty seconds," Sharon said as the private elevator dinged.

Angie hurried her steps.

"Glad you made it," Sharon called after her.

Angie sat at her desk right at nine and turned on her computer. Levi walked in before her screen had even finished waking up. He was wearing a dark navy suit today with a burgundy tie and a black dress shirt. He was stunning in anything but there was something about that navy suit that always made her daydream naughty things that involved his office chair and her on her knees. Normally he didn't even glance her way when he walked in, he'd head to his office and then in about ten minutes he'd call for coffee which she'd fetch then tell him his schedule for the day.

Today he stopped at her desk and stared at her with an intensity she hadn't seen from him since her interview a year ago. She panicked thinking he was reading her lascivious thoughts, not that there was anything new about them.

"How are you feeling?" he asked, his voice lower and more growly than usual.

Angie didn't hate the sound and it sent a little shiver up her spine. It was quickly doused by the realization that she must look terrible if he was asking her that. She wanted to shrivel up and hide from his gorgeous gaze. She couldn't meet his eyes so she raised her gaze and realized his black hair wasn't slicked back like usual. Instead, it hung dry around his face in a way that made her think he'd changed his usual routine. That didn't sit well with her. She forced a smile. "As good as always, Mr. Blackwood. You have a full schedule starting at ten. I'll bring your coffee right in."

He continued to look at her for a moment, his eyes moving down to her desk as if he were trying to see through it. What was he trying to see? He gave her a curt nod and walked away.

She jumped up as soon as he was inside his office and ran to the bathroom with her toiletry bag. She did look awful, she decided as she applied enough makeup to go from 'probably needed to stay home', to 'not looking her best'.

"You should have taken the day off, no one would have blamed you," Sharon said as Angie walked back through the lobby.

"If I hadn't had to leave the house for an appointment this morning anyway, maybe I would have. Once I was dressed and out of the house," she shrugged, "seemed a little dramatic to go back home."

"And now?" Sharon asked with a laugh.

"Now I wish I could be a little more dramatic," she admitted.

Angie fetched Levi's coffee and walked to his office, throwing her makeup bag on her desk.

Thankfully Levi didn't look at her any more than usual when she delivered it and gave him a rundown of the day's appointments. She hurried back out as fast as she could without asking if he needed anything else. When she sat at her desk again she put her head down.

She must have dozed off because she was startled by the sound of a cup being set down beside her head.

She looked up, surprised to see Patrick smiling down at her. "First hangover?"

"No, how did you know?"

"Sharon told me so I thought I'd bring you something to help."

"What is it?" she asked, eyeing the milky liquid with disdain.

"Old family recipe, did I ever tell you my great grandma was a witch?"

"No, does that mean this is magic?"

"Everyone I've ever shared it with seems to think so, gulp it."

She figured he knew more than her because despite his tales of partying on weeknights, she'd never seen him looking the way she felt.

"Cheers," Angie said and threw back the liquid. It immediately tried to come back up. She forced it back down then let loose a very unladylike gag. "Oh my god! I think I'd rather be sick."

"You'll be glad in about fifteen minutes," he assured her.

"Angelica, I need the file on the oceanfront restaurant property." Levi's voice floated out of the intercom.

Patrick looked at the closed office door. "If I were you, there's no way I would have come in today. Mr. Blackwood *and* a hangover. I'd rather drink that all day," he said motioning to the empty glass then hurried away. "If you're alive at lunch I'll buy you a coffee."

CHAPTER 4

The rest of the day went as usual except that she was brushing off questions from coworkers about what she was going to do with her bonus and feeling slightly guilty for keeping a secret from people who had become her friends over the last year. Patrick's great grandma's miracle cure did improve her symptoms after about twenty minutes and the latte he brought her at lunch did a lot too.

"I just don't understand why you wouldn't plan a vacation, especially this time of year, we get so much rain. Go somewhere tropical," Patrick said as they ate lunch in the breakroom.

"The girl doesn't need tropical, look at her skin, she'd fry," Gennie said, an accountant who spent so much time at the beach and in tanning beds that she had a year-round beach babe glow. "You should put it towards a new car."

Angie had to admit that would have been her first thought if she hadn't gone for the insemination. Her car was old and certainly on its last leg. It got her where she needed to go though, and the city had pretty good public transportation.

"Something will come up, and that's what it will be used for," she said cryptically, hoping they'd accept that she was a planner and just wanted to save. She would tell people that she was artificially inseminated, she wasn't ashamed of it, she just didn't want to announce it before she knew it was a viable pregnancy. She wasn't sure how she would explain not having the money if she didn't have the baby either. That was a problem for a future she didn't want to waste energy thinking about.

Levi walked into the breakroom then. He never came in there, at least not during lunch hours. He looked extremely out of place in his expensive suit and hesitated in the doorway.

Patrick froze with a french fry halfway to his mouth and Gennie slurped the bottom of her iced latte as they waited for him to move all the way in or demand something from one of them. Angie swallowed the bite of salad she'd been chewing as his black eyes locked onto her. "Do you need something Mr. Blackwood?" Angie asked, quickly putting the lid back on her salad.

"I—" he stopped, seeming to notice that everyone was staring at him as if he'd grown another head. "I was just wondering if the file for the Larkspring Golf clubhouse had been misplaced."

"I'll take a look. It should be in the pile of files that need looked over before next week."

He scowled. "You're on lunch, find it later." He looked like he wanted to say more but turned instead and left the room as abruptly and confusingly as he'd come in.

Angie blinked after him, unsure how to take that interaction. He'd never come looking for her before and something told her he didn't really need that file.

"Am I crazy or has that man never set foot in this room before?" Gennie said.

"Technically he only leaned in," Patrick pointed out. "He sort of *lurked* in the doorway and stared intensely at Angie." Patrick turned to look at her with a raised eyebrow.

She did *not* want to have a discussion about that look, it had been intense in a way that had made her panties damp. "I'd better go find that file." Her lunch hour was almost over anyway.

Gennie leaned close before Angie could stand up. "Is it a sex thing?"

"What?" Angie gasped.

"The *where's the clubhouse file*? Is it a secret sex code like ordering extra anchovies?"

"He's my boss," Angie gasped.

"He's hot," Gennie stated.

"He's a demon."

"He's hot," Patrick agreed.

"He's an asshole."

"He-is-*hot!*" Patrick and Gennie said in unison.

"He may be hot, but he's professional. Never once has he hit on me or made me feel uncomfortable." Angie tried not to sound disappointed by that fact. To be honest she'd had more than one daydream about walking into his office and him telling her to drop her panties and bend over his desk. Even after she realized what a demanding asshole he was, she still had those daydreams because no matter how much he asked of her as his secretary, he never crossed any lines and that made him all the more alluring to her.

He was a demon with morals.

That's when she'd started trying to date, because having the hots for your asshole boss had to be a sign of loneliness. She'd gone on a few first dates that did little to make her feel like she was out of the dry spell, and made her doubt her desirability. She'd given up for a few months then tried again hoping she could get some action before she was out of commission due to pregnancy and new motherhood. She'd gotten the action, first date car sex, then never heard from the guy again. She had no idea what it was about her that made men run after one date. She wasn't anxious to keep going through it. She hadn't had the same experience before she'd married Grayson so she assumed it was her age. Being in your late thirties wasn't exactly prime, she guessed, even if she still felt young and vibrant.

Angie walked into Levi's office and found him standing at the window with a drink in his hand. It wasn't Friday and the sight of him with an afternoon drink threw her off. He spun to face her when she entered. "Your break isn't over."

"That didn't stop you from coming to ask me a question," she pointed out and walked to the pile she knew held the clubhouse file. She located it quickly and dropped it in the middle of his desk then turned to walk out. "It wasn't misplaced. I'll head home early to make up the time." The last thing she wanted was for him to think she was a pushover. She worked a set number of hours and if he thought he could slyly insert more by interrupting her lunch, then he was mistaken. Especially with such a flimsy excuse as looking for a file that was on his desk. When she was almost to the door she saw his lunch, uneaten, sitting on the table beside the couch. She didn't say anything, just went to it and pulled the salmon and rice out of the bag. She opened the box it was in and then set it on his desk before walking out.

He said nothing as she returned to her own desk. She had left his door open, so she knew that he sat down soon after and ate his lunch. She had to bite back a grin, he always was a little extra grumpy when he didn't eat.

At four-fifty she shut off her computer, glanced at Levi's closed office door, and walked to the elevator. She was exhausted, her head was starting to pound again, and she thought maybe some greasy pizza was just the thing to ease her hungover.

"You're leaving early?" Sharon asked. She was gathering up her own things to leave.

"Yeah, Mr. Blackwood interrupted my lunch so it's only fair."

"He did, did he?" Sharon looked thoughtful.

Angie didn't have the energy to ask her what she was thinking. The elevator dinged and she got on, ready to leave the work day behind her.

. . .

Levi watched on the security feed as the elevator door shut behind Angelica. He left his office and followed as usual. Unfortunately, because Angelica had left earlier than usual, Sharon was still at her desk.

"I thought so," Sharon said slyly.

"Thought what?"

"Thought you followed that sweet girl home every night."

Levi had hired Sharon because she was a half demon and she was observant, he didn't appreciate that skill turned in his direction. He ignored her and walked into his private elevator, his thoughts fully back on Angelica. She'd been sluggish today, no doubt because of last night's celebrations. It bothered him to see her suffering and he'd almost sent her home as soon as he'd seen her that morning. He'd had to remind himself that she was an adult and could decide what was best for herself. When Patrick had brought her a drink to cure her hangover he'd kicked himself for not thinking of it first. The realization that he wanted to be the one taking care of her had been surprising and disturbing. Then at lunchtime he'd been unable to keep from checking on her and making an ass of himself in the process. He hadn't had a plan of what to say when he found her and when he had, he'd come up with a flimsy excuse that he was sure she'd seen through.

It all added up to something unexpected. He wanted her as his own. There was no denying it any longer. This wasn't just about her working for him. She was the soul he wanted to tie his life to.

As always, he took the elevator up to the penthouse then stripped out of his suit as he walked to the balcony. Demons were careful creatures, they didn't advertise all their abilities like the werewolves did, so it wasn't well known among humans that they could turn into such a devilish form. Nor that they could take flight through the night sky unseen because of their unique ability to camouflage with the darkness. Before they'd come out to humans they'd made the decision to hide these facts because of the fear they knew they were already going to face. There had been no reason to amplify humans' ideas of demons. There had been a few rumors of course and a sighting or two that went unsubstantiated. They'd come out about twenty years after the vampires and werewolves made themselves known. Demons and witches had been a little slower to step forward because they'd been burned before by overzealous humans. It turns out when they are already making movies and shows about how sexy and awesome you are, humans are much more apt to accept that you're real and that you're harmless. Things went pretty smoothly for the vampire and werewolf species and so far for demons and witches too.

His body shifted when he was through the balcony doors. His muscles bulged, his skin turned maroon and his claws sharpened into black spears. Large leathery wings sprouted out from his back and he jumped to the air, taking his well-known route to perch outside of Angelica's apartment building.

After watching her walk in with a takeout box of pizza and seeing the lights of her apartment come on, Levi hesitated. Usually he flew away, knowing Dalton would soon be stationed outside the building to keep an eye overnight. Tonight Levi felt such a pull to her that he almost went to her tiny balcony to see if he could spy in at her. He held himself back and forced himself to fly back home. He'd never invaded her privacy like that before, and he didn't intend to start tonight. It was her safety that he was after, nothing else. At least it hadn't been anything else until last night, now he was after her everything. If he didn't invade this bit of privacy of hers, would it count for anything when she found out he'd assured his sperm was used in her insemination?

He knew the answer to that and he didn't like it. Once he was back in his penthouse he dialed his brother. He needed a distraction from the fear that was tingling through him at what her reaction was going to be.

"Leviathan," Foras said smoothly. "What is this I hear about your sexy secretary making it a whole year?"

"Do you have a spy on my staff?"

"Not a spy, a friend," Foras said and Levi could hear the smile in his brother's voice.

"Yes, Angelica is still in my employ."

"Are you still holding to your no fraternization policy?"

"Of course," Levi said, teeth clenched. It wasn't a lie, he hadn't slept with the woman.

"You've spent an awful lot of time with her, you know what Mother would say about that."

"Thankfully you're the only spy she has into my life, Foras, so she won't know." Levi let a threatening note enter his tone. If their mother even thought he was showing an interest in a woman, she'd insert herself into his life to be overbearingly helpful. It was a mother demon's life goal to see her sons chosen by the most sought-after females. Levi was past the age his mother deemed suitable and so she would likely push him into courting anyone that might accept him at this point. Which is why he avoided her at all costs.

"I have to assume you are calling me because you are in need of a good time and you know your brother has the hookup in all the best clubs."

"Actually, I'm calling because I need information on demon-human pregnancies."

"Leviathan, what have you done?"

Levi knew there was no use lying to his brother. "Only assured that I can continue working with Angelica."

"You dog, I thought you didn't fuck where you work? I knew that was bullshit. What more could be expected from a demon? I'm a little proud of you. We should celebrate, want to have an orgy?"

Levi's hands clenched on the phone, he didn't like the flippant attitude toward Angelica. Foras' crass words were exactly what he'd come to expect from the man who embraced everything about being a demon.

"As I already told you, I have not slept with Angelica. I merely made sure she got my sperm instead of the random human she'd picked out at the fertility clinic."

"Oh, very demon-like behavior, brother, and very possessive. So how did she take the news?"

Levi was silent.

Foras laughed. "You haven't told her yet?"

"It was only done today, there's no guarantee the procedure even worked. I just want to be prepared, so tell me what you know."

"Why not ask Sharon?"

"Because she already knows too much of my business." Levi was fairly certain she was the one who fed information to his brother. Sharon's husband was a full demon and good friends with Foras, so the connection was there. It didn't really bother him, otherwise he would have fired her a long time ago. He didn't have any real secrets from his brother. The bigger problem was that he didn't want the office staff knowing what he'd done before he figured out what he would be telling Angelica. And Sharon liked to talk to everyone. He doubted Foras relayed information back to Sharon so this seemed like a safe option.

"I have heard that they grow rather quickly compared to human babies. You know a demon pregnancy lasts around three months, and humans go for nine. Half demons born to humans tend to be around six months and half demons born to demons are the usual three."

"Six months," Levi mumbled with a frown. That didn't give him much time to figure out how to tell her what had happened. Or to figure out a way to get her to move out of her dangerous and tiny apartment and in with him. Suddenly he knew he would accept nothing less. He wanted her in his home where he could care for her.

"Can I be there when you tell Mom?"

"No, and if you mention it to her, I will hunt you down and cut off your favorite appendage."

"Yikes, okay fine. Don't wait too long, I have a tendency to talk when I'm drunk, which is often, and always when mother is around."

Levi hung up on his brother. The distraction hadn't served him well, he was still obsessing over Angelica and the distance between them. He stared out at the night and debated his options. In the end the only thing he knew, was that he needed to keep her closer. He needed her here. Her building wasn't fit for anyone so it opened up an easy opportunity. When she'd first started working for him he'd briefly looked into buying the building. Mr. Miller, the man who owned it, wasn't interested in selling at the time and Levi hadn't been motivated to pressure him. Partly because he'd expected Angelica to only last a month, tops. He had still made a few vague threats about codes and standards to the owner because everyone deserved a decent place to live their life. The man had made some minor improvements to the place in the last year. It was still no place that a baby should be raised in and he would never allow his own offspring to be brought up in a place like that. All valid reasons to get Angelica out of there.

Maybe it was time to pay Mr. Miller another visit.

CHAPTER 5

Angie woke up feeling great compared to the day before. Still a little tired but at least it was Friday. She followed her usual morning routine which was a quick yoga workout, breakfast and shower. She dressed in black slacks and a cute white top, threw on a purple cardigan and then she was out the door with time to spare.

She froze on the stoop outside her building when she saw Levi talking to the owner, Mr. Miller. The juxtaposition of the two men was almost comical. Mr. Miller was barely taller than herself and quite round. He had a dark complexion and no hair on his head though he kept a black mustache that was far too bushy in her opinion. His eyes were a gold brown and always darting around as if he noticed everything. As usual, he wore khaki slacks and a red polo shirt with his company logo on it. Next to him Levi looked like a million-dollar bachelor, which she assumed he was. He wore a black suit today with a white button up and a black tie. It was what he wore whenever he had an important meeting, she'd noticed throughout the year. Why was he wearing it to meet with Mr. Miller? Panic welled up inside her at the possibility that this was going to be one of Blackwood

Construction's next projects. Why else would Levi be here, or Mr. Miller, he only came around to collect late rent. There was no way she'd believe Mr. Miller was trying to hire Levi's company to do work on the building, they did high-end renovations and new builds. She hadn't been with Blackwood Construction long enough to know if this was the sort of thing they would be interested in taking on as a sort of charity case. More likely they would buy it cheap then knock it down to build something expensive. The building was slightly rundown, though nothing broken was ever left that way for long. It could use a little paint, other than that, it was probably the nicest building in the neighborhood. It was better even than a year ago when she'd moved in. She had expected her rent to go up when Mr. Miller started doing minor renovations that had her neighbors mumbling with suspicious joy. It hadn't though and she'd been grateful.

"Angelica, perfect timing. Can you schedule a meeting with Mr. Miller in the office next week? We have urgent business to discuss."

Angie could only blink and nod as Levi addressed her with no surprise. Had he known she lived here?

"Of course," Angie hurried to agree and dug around in her purse for her phone.

Levi nodded at Mr. Miller then turned and walked to his waiting car, a sleek black thing that looked entirely out of place on this street. He got into the driver's seat but didn't drive away.

"What would be good for you?" she asked Mr. Miller as she opened the calendar app.

Mr. Miller looked at her skeptically, his gaze running from her face down her body and back up in a way that made her skin crawl. His mouth was set in a line that said he wasn't seeing anything special about her. "Mr. Blackwood is still your boss?"

"Yes, I haven't changed jobs." She had to pause then because she didn't remember ever telling him where she worked. She had been looking for work when she first rented the apartment and all they'd cared about was if she could pay the security deposit and first and last month's rent at the time.

"I'll come in on Tuesday," Mr. Miller said before Angie could ask how he knew where she worked.

"Sure, let me see what times are available." She scheduled him for Tuesday afternoon then walked across the street and tapped on Levi's window. "Mr. Blackwood?"

The window rolled down just enough for his voice to clearly reach her. "Get in, I'll give you a ride to work."

"I have a car." she said automatically, dumbstruck by this entirely out of character event.

"I am aware. I want to drive you to work before we're both late," he snapped.

"Then I'll have to get a ride home tonight. It's better if I just take my car, I won't be late, I'm parked right there." She motioned to her car which was old, small, and really needed a wash. It was almost embarrassing to admit it was hers while he was sitting in a car that was probably worth more than the house she'd owned with Grayson.

"I'll get you home."

"No, that's not necessary," she tried.

He rolled up his window, essentially cutting off any further argument. Angie did not want to get in the car with him, it was too familiar, and far too close. Did she really want to push the issue though? The offer itself was nice, even if he was being heavy-handed about it. She watched him look at his watch in annoyance and she rushed around to get in the car. Making them both late with her indecision wasn't something she wanted to do.

She sank down onto soft leather seats and put her bag on the floor by her feet. There wasn't a speck of dirt on the mats and she bit her lip, feeling like she should have wiped her feet before she got in. She knew he was a clean man, not obsessive about it, he just liked things neat and always in their place. It had been a struggle for her not to clutter her desk after noticing in the first week there that he glared at anything extra laying on it.

"Buckle up," he said and she hurried to comply. It wasn't until they'd pulled away from the curb that she realized she had missed seeing Dalton. Likely he'd been scared off by Mr. Miller's presence, not wanting to be accused of loitering.

As they drove, the faint scent of sweet smoke reached her. It was familiar and not unpleasant. It felt weird to be smelling her boss so clearly, and she knew it was him because she'd caught whiffs of it ever since the first day she'd met him. It had never been this strong before and she assumed it was embedded into the car interior. Maybe he smoked in the car. She'd never actually seen him smoke a cigar, but the smell was unmistakable. She actually really liked it, which was disturbing to her in a very pleasurable way.

Her body heated and her head started to whirl a little. Riding with him was definitely a bad idea. She reached for the temperature control and his hand got there first. She jerked away instinctively, as if touching his hand would burn. Maybe it would, she wasn't sure what demons were like beyond really demanding in the workplace and that didn't scare her like it did at first. Even with all the time they'd spent together in the last year, she'd never so much as brushed fingers with Levi when passing a paper. Suddenly she couldn't help but wonder about his body temperature and what it would feel like all over her skin. Obviously the heat and stress was causing temporary insanity.

Soon the fresh air conditioning was blasting on her and she leaned forward so it could hit directly on her face.

"Thank you," she said.

He didn't respond, just drove on in silence.

Angie didn't do well with silence. "What are you and Mr. Miller meeting about exactly? I wasn't sure what to put in the calendar notes," she said as an excuse to prove she wasn't just being nosy.

"He wants to sell the building."

"Oh no! Where will I go?" Panic bubbled up. She knew she was going to have to move in the next nine months, but this could mean she'd need to move soon. She hadn't saved a deposit up yet. Not to mention the other people in the building who likely didn't have the resources to move, otherwise why would they be there? Mrs. Levinson who was older than dirt and lived alone on the bottom floor had no living relatives and she was on a fixed income. Clara Bradley and her two young boys would probably have to go live with her parents in Washington, a fate Angie knew the woman had been avoiding because she loathed her small hometown. Mr. and Mrs. Yantz had just moved in and were saving money to buy a house and start a family. "It's not fair," she proclaimed, throwing him a scowl. "People live there."

"I didn't say it was getting condemned, although it wouldn't surprise me, the place is a dump."

"It's the nicest dump in the neighborhood."

"Right, he's done some work recently," Levi admitted.

Angie was surprised he knew that. Had he been watching the building for a while and planning to buy it? "You've done this in the past, haven't you? You bought old cheap buildings and torn them down to build something you can make money off of?"

"Yes."

"So…" Angie prompted.

He sighed as if answering her questions was a great annoyance. "That would be the best scenario for that space. It could really uplift the whole neighborhood to have new condos there."

"Or it could drive prices up in the whole neighborhood. You do realize people live there because it's all they can afford, right?" Angie crossed her arms over her chest and glared at the side of his face. In that moment she didn't care that he was her boss, she was going to defend the entire neighborhood from his greedy intrusion.

"I'm in the business of making money, not people happy."

"Where will we go?" she whispered, her voice hitching a little with emotion. She dropped her arms as the helplessness of it sank in. If Mr. Miller wanted to sell and Levi wanted to buy, there was nothing to stop it.

He looked at her with a scowl. "I'm certain that everyone will find a place."

"Easy for you to say, you have more money than god, we live there because we're dirt poor."

"I pay you well," Levi defended.

"Yeah, but this city isn't cheap."

Levi fell silent at that.

Angie didn't have to stay in the city now that she'd been inseminated. She could go anywhere. Somewhere small and cheap, somewhere with seasons and a quiet atmosphere to raise a child in. She liked the city though, and she even liked her job most of the time. None of that mattered if she couldn't provide for her child. Maybe this was the push she needed to make a big move and be near her sister in Montana. Angie sighed and looked out the passenger window.

"What are you thinking about?" Levi demanded.

"Excuse me?" Angie turned and raised an eyebrow in his direction. She didn't owe him an explanation.

He cleared his throat. "You sighed, I'd like to know why." His tone was more curious than demanding so she answered.

"I was thinking that I could move to a small town in Montana since there's nothing holding me here. I just signed a new lease at the apartment but if that's about to be dissolved, literally, then I suppose I can do whatever, go wherever. My sister has been asking me to move closer to her and her husband ever since my divorce."

"You want to leave Larkspring?" he asked, his tone deadly calm.

She didn't trust that tone. It was the one he used in business meetings that weren't going his way and were about to. His back was ramrod straight, his jaw was clenched so tight a vein was popping out, and his knuckles had gone white on the steering wheel.

"This is usually where I offer to get you a drink," she said dryly.

He looked at her incredulous. "Pardon?"

"In meetings when you get that tone and that stiff look, I usually ask if you or your guest need a refill on refreshment. It defuses the situation." She dug in her purse.

"You think you *handle* me?" he asked, a hint of amusement in his voice.

"Not at all. Mint?" she asked, holding out the small tin from her purse.

His body looked completely relaxed as he grabbed one and stuck it in his mouth. Angie tried not to stare at his lips as he did. She couldn't help herself, he had really nice lips for a guy. They weren't too thin or puffy, just perfectly kissable and tinted dusty pink. She imagined he'd taste slightly smoky and sweet.

She shook herself and forced her gaze back to the street, those were *not* thoughts she should have about her boss. Especially since he was about to be the reason she had to move.

Levi couldn't get Angelica's comment out of his head. All day he kept thinking back on every meeting he'd had since she'd started working for him. Ninety percent of the time he had her sit in to take notes on her laptop. The first time she'd offered to refresh drinks for him and his guest had surprised him, it quickly became normalized. He never put together that she did it when he started to get especially irritated with the person he was meeting with. Though now that he thought about it, he hadn't had an explosive meeting since she started, so maybe she was on to something.

What else did she do that he hadn't noticed? He couldn't imagine there was much since he noticed everything she did and everywhere she was. He couldn't *not* notice her. She was smart and sexy and she'd somehow managed to deal with him for over a year, she was amazing.

When he approached her at five-o'clock to take her home she was cleaning off her desk. He watched as she opened a drawer and swept the desk free of pens, pencils and notes. The drawer was an unorganized junk pile and he cringed when she shut it and stood.

"Ready," she said brightly.

"Is that your method of organization?"

She looked at him confused, then down at the drawer she'd just closed. "Oh, yeah I know you don't like clutter so I put it in the drawer."

"But how do you know what's important? How do you find what you need?"

"Mr. Blackwood have I ever forgotten an appointment?"

"No."

"Have I ever misplaced a file?"

"No."

"A client message ever been undelivered?"

"Not that I'm aware."

"Then I guess my method of organization works just fine."

Levi could only grunt.

Angelica looked smug as she grabbed her purse and walked around the desk. Levi followed her to the lobby. She was wearing slacks today and his eyes were glued to her ass as it swung down the hall.

Sharon was already gone from her desk and Levi was thankful he didn't have to deal with her knowing looks. The elevator ride was packed with other employees heading home for the day, all of them gave him curious looks while making small talk with Angelica. It annoyed him that they all seemed on such good terms with her, even employees from the businesses he rented out on other levels of the building seemed to know her and greet her familiarly. He had the urge to grab her and whisk her away where no one else could look at her. His demon instincts to covet and keep were rearing up strong and he didn't know how to handle it. He felt his body start to heat and moved uncomfortably as he reigned himself back in.

"I can call a ride," Angie insisted when they stepped off in the parking garage.

"You need a ride home?" Patrick asked, having come off the elevator at the same time. "You live on my way; I can give you a ride."

"That would be great, thanks. I don't want to make Mr. Blackwood drive across town for no reason."

Levi felt a rumble of disagreement start in his chest. How could he argue? They all knew he lived here so there was no valid reason for him to take her home when someone else was offering. If he could quiet the pounding of his blood maybe he could think of a valid excuse. Perhaps a place near her building that he was heading to in order to make him taking her make sense. He couldn't, and the look of relief on Angie's face at the new plan was like a stake to the heart. All Levi could do was grunt and walk to the private elevator that took him directly to the top floor where he lived.

For the first time in all the years he'd been there, he felt a yearning ache at the emptiness of his home when he stepped off the elevator.

CHAPTER 6

"So you rode to work with the boss man today?" Patrick asked as soon as they were in his truck.

"It was weird. He was outside my building talking to the owner this morning, then insisted we save the environment and share a ride."

"Oh shit, is he buying your building?"

"They have a meeting on Tuesday," she groaned.

"What are you going to do?"

"Move obviously."

"Does that mean your bonus is going to be spent on moving expenses?"

"Definitely not." Because she'd already spent it and she had no money left for moving.

"That's good. Do you have any fun weekend plans? It's Friday night, we could grab a drink before I drop you off."

"I'm not sure I ever want to drink again," she laughed. It wasn't a lie, just the thought of alcohol made her heave slightly. "What are your wild weekend plans?"

"I'm going to meet a friend for a movie tonight and tomorrow I'll probably hit up a few clubs, dance all my troubles away."

"What kind of troubles do you have?"

"Not about to lose my apartment troubles, which makes me think you should come dancing with me."

"I'll call you tomorrow if I have the energy," she lied as he stopped in front of her building. She wasn't interested in getting drunk or laid so there was no reason to go to the types of places Patrick frequented.

Angie waved her friend away and hurried inside. She spent the weekend at home wondering if she was pregnant and if she was going to be kicked out of her apartment without enough money for a deposit on a new place. All the stress made her wish she could have gone out for a drink and dancing. Since she couldn't, it was just her and her thoughts for two days. She did finish crocheting a small baby blanket though in a nice yellow and cream so it was neutral.

By Monday Angie was excited to get back to work and real distractions.

Levi paid careful attention to Angelica on Monday. He knew from Dalton's report that she hadn't left her apartment all weekend except to do a grocery run. It wasn't her normal routine. She usually had some kind of weekend outing planned with someone from work or even alone. She often took the short drive to Oceanview where she would get coffee at a little werewolf-owned shop and drink it on the beach. The first time he'd heard about it he had assumed she was meeting someone. Then he followed her himself the next time and she really was just enjoying herself. It was a skill to be comfortable alone, and apparently she had it. Though he imagined she was avoiding being around anyone right now because she didn't want anyone to ask too many questions about the bonus. It didn't seem like she was telling everyone about the insemination just yet. He wished he could have told her that he knew. Then he could have offered to spend time with her because she didn't have to hide anything from him. Of course *he* wasn't ready to admit what he'd done either.

On Monday she seemed happy and while he was observing her more closely he realized that she did quite a lot for him outside of what he required of a secretary. She anticipated so many of his needs from morning coffee to afternoon tea every day. It made him think over what else she did, like having his drycleaning slung over a chair on Friday morning and fresh ice in his bucket because she knew on Fridays he liked an afternoon whiskey rather than tea. He had taken all these things for granted in the last year. She'd gradually learned his habits until he didn't even ask for things any longer and didn't appreciate that he didn't have to.

Which made him an asshole.

He tried to name as many things that he did for her and other than paying her a more than reasonable salary, he couldn't think of much. He kept her safe, had made sure that her apartment building was livable, and he kept her employed. It didn't feel like enough. If she were a demon woman she'd demand he prove his devotion daily. That was the way that a male won a mate against other suitors. Once won, the devotion didn't end, a male would continue to care for and provide for his mate and any children they produced. If they stopped providing to her satisfaction, the female was within her rights to find another more suitable mate.

He knew he'd gone about things the wrong way with Angelica because he'd panicked. Now he had to deal with the consequences. That didn't mean he couldn't do things the right way now. He just had to prove himself to her without scaring her off. How did you prove yourself to someone without declaring your intentions? Or admitting what you'd already done?

Angelica was going to kill him when she found out. *If* there was anything to find out. He knew there was still a chance that the insemination hadn't worked, although when you involve a witch, and apparently a goddess, the chances were almost certain. He'd still wait until she was surely pregnant before he revealed what he'd done. It would give him time to come up with a reasonable plan and deal with Miller. His decision to buy the building was still a good business move and would do wonders for the neighborhood, no matter if she was pregnant or not.

Despite what she may think of him, he wasn't heartless. He'd be sure that all the residents of Miller's building were taken care of after he bought it. His plan was to offer them all enough time and money to relocate without stress, then he would raze the building and build something that offered low-income housing as well as a few shops on the bottom floor. He'd done it elsewhere and it had turned out great. Plus it was good P.R. for him, and a tax break.

On Tuesday morning he cut his gym routine short to purchase some herbal teas and set them on her desk. If she was pregnant, she'd have to cut out the caffeine. He'd seen her drink tea in the past so it seemed like a reasonable choice that wouldn't give away what he knew. Then he left the office before she arrived so she wouldn't be thrown off by a change in routine.

"Why are you here so early sneaking around?" Sharon asked. She'd just sat at her desk as he was heading back to his elevator.

"Needed to drop something off," he mumbled.

She made a thoughtful noise which he ignored and headed back upstairs.

He arrived back on the office floor a few minutes later at his normal time and ignored Sharon's pointed look. He slowed down as he was passing Angelica's desk. She was stunning in a black fitted dress today. Her hair was up in a bun with a few tendrils falling around her face making her look soft in a way that caused an ache in his chest. He had a sudden urge to tug those tendrils and watch them bounce back up. He fisted his hands to keep from reaching out.

"Good morning Mr. Blackwood. Do you know where this

came from? Are you switching to tea?" She held up one of the tea boxes.

"Oh, uh. No, I put it there because I thought you might like it."

"Thanks," she said, confusion in her tone that made his face heat with embarrassment. He hurried to his office and closed the door. It wasn't the reaction he wanted, of course expecting her to throw herself at him in appreciation of tea was delusional, though it had crossed his mind. If only she knew how long he'd stood in the tea aisle and stared at the choices before picking those.

Levi watched her closely all morning to see what other needs she may have. He needed to know what he could do for her. There was nothing that he could tell. She was infuriatingly independent. At lunch he went to offer to order something for her and she was already walking to the staff lounge with her packed lunch.

On Wednesday he put fresh fruit in the staff lounge, hoping to supplement her lunch needs. He wasn't about to make the same mistake of showing up in there during lunch to check if she was eating it though, so he had no idea if she even got any before the rest of the staff had some. He'd debated putting it on her desk, except her awkwardness around the tea told him that was not the best idea.

On Thursday he had a new desk chair delivered to her that was more ergonomic according the saleswoman.

"I don't need a new chair," Angelica said with a frown when it showed up.

"That one is quite old and I'm upgrading everyone's."

"Sharon should be first, she's been here the longest. Why don't I take this out to her," Angelica said, already moving the chair down the hall.

"No," Levi bellowed, his body heating.

Angelica froze and turned to face him with wide eyes.

"That chair is for you, I have a different one coming for

Sharon," he snarled and walked to his office, slamming the door shut. As soon as he was calm, he ordered a chair for Sharon.

On Friday he was at a loss for ideas and watched her leave for the day, feeling like a failure. He headed upstairs a few minutes later intending to follow as usual.

He hated that he wouldn't see her over the next couple of days. Usually, it didn't bother him more than the thought of whether or not she was safe. Today it felt like the weekend was an impossible task he had to get through. Two days where he couldn't prove himself to her, and he couldn't see her, or smell her sweet scent.

He couldn't assess every little thing as a possible sign of pregnancy.

Levi found Foras leaning against his front door and his mood went from self-wallowing pity to annoyance.

He much preferred annoyance. "Why in hell are you here?"

"I was bored and thought you might like to entertain me."

"I wouldn't," Levi said, unlocking his door.

Foras was unbothered by his attitude and followed him inside. "Are we going to a bar or a club?" Foras asked.

"Neither."

"Boring."

"Yes, which is why you should leave."

"No chance. Mom wants a full report because you haven't called this week."

"Of course she sent you," Levi groaned. "Tell her I'm great."

"Nope, I can't lie to her. She would boil me alive if she found out. I'll stay the weekend and tell her the truth. You're a lovesick fool who got his secretary pregnant."

"I don't know for sure yet," Levi said between gritted teeth.

"About which part?" Foras asked with a grin.

Levi gritted his teeth harder and sent a message to Dalton. It was going to be a very long weekend.

Not wanting to spend two days alone with his brother and all his probing questions, Levi agreed to go out with Foras to a vampire bar. If he was lucky, Foras would find a woman to spend the rest of the weekend with.

"I know you're sad that you can't stalk your secretary right now, but try to look less like you want to kill everyone or they won't let us in," Foras ordered as they approached Sundown Saloon, a cowboy-themed vampire bar. "Trust me, you'll have a good time in here, Jason recommended it."

Levi was familiar with Jason Vandean and his sister Sara who was a wiz at public relations, he'd used her services early in building his company. They were well connected vampires in the city and Foras and Jason had been friends for years. Levi didn't have anything against the guy, but he wasn't in the mood to be social.

A large werewolf bouncer sniffed in their direction with a growl. "Demons," he stated and moved to let them in.

"They don't let humans in unless they're with a vampire, it helps keep everyone safe," Foras said as they strode into the dark-lit room. It was decorated to look like an old saloon complete with a piano on a stage where a woman in costume was singing loudly, and not very well in Levi's opinion. There were mostly vampires in the bar judging by the pale skin and red-brown eyes he caught sight of. A few possible humans were mixed in, always hanging close to a vampire, so obviously a date. At least one group of werewolves was present who looked like they might be celebrating something. It was all typical for a vampire bar and Levi knew that most of what was being consumed in the bar was blood, some mixed with liquor. In the past he'd come to a place like this and find a woman willing to go home with him for the night, or maybe just to his car. Tonight he looked at all the exposed skin and curious eyes with no interest, not a single stirring of his blood or body. It had been the same for a year. No one interested him since Angelica had walked into his office.

"Want to join a poker game or just drink?" Foras asked. He

looked around the room with glittering eyes, ready to indulge in everything being offered.

Before Levi could reply they were greeted enthusiastically by Jason. "Hey! The Blackwood brothers."

"Jason, good to see you man," Foras gave the vampire a quick back slap hug.

"Levi, your brother said you need a drink or four."

"I guess he's right," Levi agreed and followed the two friends to a table.

"I hear you're looking at a new hotel build on the waterfront," Jason said after they all had drinks in front of them.

"I am."

Jason sipped his drink and raised an eyebrow at Levi's short answer.

"My brother is lovesick," Foras explained.

Levi snarled.

Jason laughed. "It happens to the best men," he joked. "Lost my best friend to a wonderful woman about a year and a half ago."

"Saw that. A human too, isn't she?" Foras pressed.

Levi perked up a bit, he knew who they were talking about, Viktor Paulie. They'd used the clinic that Angelica had gone to.

"Happy as hell now, with their little family," Jason said with a sigh.

Foras shook his head. "No way, I'll stay single." He looked around the room. "In fact, I'm going to make a round and see if I can drum us up some lady friends."

"Don't," Levi said.

"Fine, just for me then." Foras stood and wandered to the crowd.

Levi turned to Jason. "Everything worked out for them then? There was nothing in the news after the birth announcement and Johnson praising the clinic for helping his son."

"Everything was perfect, it was destiny," Jason said.

A knot untied in Levi's chest, he wasn't sure if he believed in destiny but what else could he call the draw he'd felt to Angelica? He finished his drink and looked around, Foras was likely in some dark corner with a vampire's fangs in his neck while he shoved a hand up her skirt.

"Tell Foras I left, if he even bothers to come back and look for me."

"Will do, and good luck with your girl," Jason said, lifting his glass in salute.

Levi wasted no time getting out of there and then he drove to Angelica's building. He had to check on her.

Foras' stalker comment ran through his mind but he didn't care, he couldn't stay away. Dalton was there of course and assured him that Angelica hadn't left since she'd gotten home from work.

"I'm just going to check on her, she seemed off today," Levi lied.

Dalton didn't seem to buy it, only smirked at him and sat back down.

Levi walked around to the side of the building and peered up at the second floor balcony he knew was hers. Safe in the shadow he took off his jacket and shirt then let his wings sprout. It was a dangerous sort of form for him, because he wasn't activating his camouflage coloring, only the wings. Anyone could see him if he wasn't careful, but this was the only way he could fly without getting fully nude. Being caught with his pants down outside her window would be worse than letting out a demon secret.

A couple of flaps and he was up on level with her windows. There she was, sitting on her couch surrounded by blankets and pillows with a mug in her hands and the television on. She looked half asleep and perfectly fine.

Every instinct told him to rush forward, to go through her balcony door and be with her. Coming here had been a mistake, it didn't ease his worry, it amplified his desire.

His phone rang in his pocket and he dropped down just as her head turned to look outside.

"Shit," he hissed and grabbed his shirt. He pulled his phone out, seeing Foras' face there. "What?" he answered.

"You are stalking her, aren't you?"

"I told you I wasn't interested in cheap women and bad music," he snapped back, pulling his shirt on and walking from the alley. He waved at Dalton as he went to his car, Foras giving him all the reasons why he should be at the bar with him.

"And besides, I need a ride, you abandoned me."

"Jason can give you a ride."

"He's occupied and I am supposed to be making sure you're okay."

"Tell mother to mind her own business."

Foras' laughed and Levi hung up. He drove home knowing he would likely get a visit from his mother soon as a result, but he couldn't care. The only thing he could care about was Angelica and how he was going to make her his, permanently. His demon instincts would accept nothing less, not now that he was admitting, at least to himself, that he wanted to court her. He wanted to prove he was worthy of her attention, then her affection and finally, worthy of her commitment. He wanted what he thought he'd never want, to be chosen by a female.

CHAPTER 7

Angie woke up on Monday, sweating. Hot flashes like nothing she'd ever experienced in her life had been plaguing her all weekend. She knew it could be a pregnancy symptom, but she thought it would have taken longer to get any. She also felt nauseous to the point where she could hardly eat the last two days and her breasts were so tender she debated whether or not she could go braless at work. She decided absolutely not with her luscious Ds.

Knowing it was likely too soon to be pregnancy-related and not willing to risk her chances of conceiving because of the flu, she made an appointment with an OBGYN. Then she called in sick to work for the first time. Technically she sent an email to Sharon who was the unfortunate one who had to fill in for her. Sharon would also have to be the one to let Levi know she was out when he arrived. She doubted it would affect his day very much. It was likely to ruin Sharon's unfortunately.

Since she wasn't going to work, she dressed for how she felt, awful. She pulled on some sweats and a loose T-shirt over a tank top that she decided was an adequate substitute for a bra today. She pulled her red curls up into a bun, skipped makeup, and walked out of the house with a water bottle. If she sipped slowly it wouldn't make her want to vomit.

"Woah, Ms. Walsh, you look like shit."

"Thanks Dalton, good to see you, too."

"Did you stay up drinking again last night? Is this a new thing? Party girl at your age isn't a good look."

She scowled at Dalton and was about to tell him where he could shove his opinion. Bile rising in her throat stopped the words. She turned and unloaded her stomach over the side of the stoop.

"Shit, should I call someone?"

"No, I'm heading to the doctor."

"You don't look well enough to drive, let me take you."

"You have a car?" She was shocked because he seemed to spend most of his time sitting outside her apartment building. When did he work to afford a car?

"Yeah, I got a car. Come on." He offered her his arm and she was unsteady enough to take it.

"You're not trying to lure me into your car so you can drink my blood are you?"

He laughed. "Nope, I am in a committed blood relationship, your veins are safe with me."

She wasn't sure if she should believe that or not, but she was too sick to care. "You aren't usually here this late in the day," she said as they walked around the corner.

"Yeah, I guess I didn't have anything to go do this morning."

"But the sun's been out for a while, is there enough shade for you on the stoop?"

He smiled at her concern. "Yeah, it's fine, you don't have to worry about me." His phone rang and he pulled it out of his pocket. He glanced at the screen then silenced it and stuck it back, then a couple steps later it rang again.

"Should you get that?"

"Nah, I'll call him back."

He led her to a newer car that had been enhanced with stickers along the sides and a spoiler on the back. Its windows were tinted so dark she couldn't see anything inside, even the windshield had a layer on it that would make driving dangerous for her. She knew it protected a vampire from too much sun. It was a nice car, it reminded her of when The Fast and The Furious was popular. "Are you a big Vin Diesel fan?"

"Ladies like it," he said with a coy smile and a shrug.

He helped her into the passenger seat, which was small. Thankfully she was short. The interior was clean and had so many knobs and buttons she was sure it must fly or something. It was definitely expensive and she was once again concerned that Dalton was spending his days doing something illegal.

"Where to?" Dalton asked when he sat behind the wheel.

She gave him the address and brief directions. Her own phone rang as they weaved through traffic and she saw it was Levi. She had no interest in answering. She deserved a sick day and whatever he needed could be handled by Sharon, or it could wait until tomorrow when she was feeling better.

Dalton pulled to a stop in front of the clinic she'd directed him to. "I'll wait here and drive you home after."

"You don't have to. I don't know how long it'll be and I can call a ride."

He pulled out his phone and shrugged. "I'll be here."

Angie wasn't sure why he was being so nice. She decided she'd pay him for the ride when they got back to her building. There was no reason he should be acting as her chauffeur, though she *was* glad she hadn't had to drive herself while feeling so sick.

When Angie entered the building she felt a rise of panic. What if something was wrong? What if the pregnancy wasn't viable, or it was ectopic? So many things could be going on and she could be about to find out that all of her hopes were gone. And she was alone with that fear because she was doing this on her own which meant she would be alone with the results too. She didn't have any friends close enough to call in for this sort of thing, only her sister who was too far away to be here physically. Maybe she should have moved to Montana after the divorce. Except there were no witch-run fertility clinics in Montana.

Tears prickled her eyes as she checked in with the receptionist, then sat down. She pulled out her phone, ignoring the missed calls and texts from Levi, and texted her sister.

I'm in the doctor's office, I think something might be wrong.

Henley's reply was immediate.

Can you talk?

No, I'm in the waiting room. I'll call as soon as I'm out.

Okay, want me to fly down there?

Angie knew Henley really would fly down if Angie needed her, it wasn't just a polite offer. They were each other's only family, their parents had passed away a few years ago and they didn't have any living grandparents or close relatives. They talked a lot and shared everything that was going on in their lives. Henley and her husband had even helped Angie move when she got her divorce while trying to convince her to come live with them.

Don't buy a ticket yet, I'll call you when I'm out of here, I just needed someone to know.

. . .

I understand.

Angie tucked her phone back in her purse and tried not to look too closely at all the pregnant women around her. She so badly wanted to be one of them. A few tears slipped silently down her face before she could wipe them away. She didn't do well with expressing her emotions in public and she really didn't want the pitying looks that were being shot her way. So, she took a breath, steeled herself for whatever was about to happen, and waited to be called back.

It was only a few minutes before a nurse wearing red scrubs and a big smile called her name. Angie followed the woman back to a room where she was asked a million questions and her vitals were taken. Then she was instructed to strip from the waist down and sit on the exam table.

This wasn't her first time in this office so she knew the routine. She'd been seeing Dr. Brunswick over the last year in preparation for the insemination. When the tall, mid-fifties woman walked in with a look of concern, Angie stopped trying to hold herself together.

"I know something's wrong," Angie said through fresh tears.

"We don't know anything, Angie, but we will find out. You had the insemination?"

"Yes. It's too soon to test, and way too soon to have symptoms. That's how I know something's wrong."

"Or you might have the flu. Your temperature is elevated and you told the nurse you've been nauseous. I am going to do a test for influenza after we take a look at what is happening in your womb right now."

"Isn't it too early for that?"

"Unfortunately it's too early to do it the easy way, which is why you had to take your bottoms off. We'll do an internal ultrasound and see if we can find anything going on."

Angie was comforted by the woman's even tone and reasonable words. She laid back and put her feet in the stirrups as Dr. Brunswick got things ready.

"This isn't the most comfortable procedure, but it shouldn't hurt. Tell me if you feel anything other than a little pressure. I'm hoping to see implantation today. If not, I don't want you to freak out because it is still early."

Dr. Brunswick inserted the wand and the attending nurse turned a dark screen toward Angie.

"Okay, I'm prepared to not know anything today," Angie assured her. Mentally she wasn't prepared at all, she needed reassurance or she was going to continue freaking out.

"Have you had any spotting or—" The doctor froze, staring at the screen.

Angie's panic spiked. There was a blur on the screen that she couldn't take her eyes off of even though she had no idea what she was looking at.

"When did you get the insemination?"

"Week before last, it's been like ten days."

"Is there any chance you got pregnant before that?"

"No, I mean I had a date but we used protection. That was like three or four weeks ago."

"Yeah … I think it didn't work."

Angie closed her eyes and took a deep breath. It didn't work, she wasn't pregnant and she was out of money. There was no bonus coming and she was out of options. There was nothing to do now but accept that she would never give birth to her own child. "Okay, well that's okay, maybe I can adopt," she said on a sob.

"No, I mean you're definitely pregnant. It looks like you're about three weeks pregnant, not two. Which would make more sense given your symptoms of nausea. The low fever I'm still worried about, but you're pregnant. The condom didn't work."

"Fuck," Angie said as a myriad of emotions ran through her.

The guy she'd gone on one okay date with and had never heard from again after they'd fucked in his car outside the bar, was Mike. She was pregnant and it was Mike's baby. He must have some super sperm, that and the fact that she'd been on some fertility increasing drugs at the time preparing for insemination must have worked magic. She couldn't even really be mad about it because in the end she was getting a baby, the thing she'd dreamed about for so long.

She looked at the blur again and recognized it for what it was, her dreams come true.

Dr. Brunswick took some blood and swabbed her throat to check for illnesses, then she prescribed something for the nausea and sent her away with instructions to rest and drink plenty of fluids. Angie stopped at the reception desk to make a follow up appointment and couldn't keep the smile from her face. The receptionist beamed back at her.

"I'm glad to see you're feeling better, Ms. Walsh."

"Thank you, I am."

Angie left in a daze, her joy hindered only by the new complication of Mike. She wasn't sure what to do. On one hand she'd expected to do this thing on her own so was there any reason to contact the guy who had been avoiding her like the plague since they slept together? Then again she knew how important it was to her to be a parent and so she wouldn't want to keep that choice away from anyone else. If he didn't want to have anything to do with the child that was no big deal. She knew she'd need to at least let him know what was happening though and give him the option.

Angie was surprised to see that Dalton was still in the parking lot waiting for her. When he spotted her, he hopped out of his car and hurried around it to open the passenger door.

"You waited," she stated dumbly.

He shrugged as if it were no big deal. "I said I would."

"Yeah, but don't you have something more important to be doing? I am capable of calling for a ride."

"Nope, nothing. So you need to go anywhere before we head back to your apartment?"

"Could you stop at the pharmacy? I have to grab a prescription and I want to buy some crackers and ginger tea."

"Sure thing." He shut the door when she was seated and strolled around to his side of the car, pulling out his phone to type out a text. He stood outside the driver's door for a few minutes, apparently waiting for a reply. When he got in the car he had his lips pressed together and his eyebrows pulled down. "You pregnant?"

"I am," she said and the joy of it was too much to contain. No reason to lie to him or anyone else now.

"On purpose then? You aren't freaking out, just sick? My mom was super sick with my little sister, puked every day for months I swear."

"Yeah, on purpose."

"And the lucky guy is..."

"None of your business."

"Sure. Well, I hope he knows he's lucky to lock down someone like you."

"He doesn't know."

"You gonna tell him?" Dalton asked with no judgment.

"Yeah, I think he deserves to know. I don't need him to do anything about it though if he doesn't want to."

"That's cool."

CHAPTER 8

Levi was relieved when he got the message from Dalton saying that Angelica was tucked away safely at home. And he ignored the not-so-subtle questions about who the father of the child Angelica was carrying was. It was uncharacteristic of Dalton to probe like that and it annoyed Levi, the man was supposed to watch her for him, not be her friend. Levi was even annoyed that Dalton had taken her to the appointment today, though he was glad Angelica hadn't driven herself. It sounded like she was in pretty bad shape. Levi wanted to be the one to drive her when she was upset or sick and it grated on him that another man had done it. His body started to heat with the anger and he knew he wasn't getting any more work done today. He got himself under control and walked out of his office.

He thought he was hiding his agitation well, until Sharon scowled at him and told him he was smoking and his skin was darkening.

"Shit," Levi grumbled and took a few breaths before anyone else noticed. The last thing he wanted to do was go up in flames or start to shift forms in front of his employees. Even if they knew what he was, he tried not to shove it in their faces. It didn't do him any good to have them fear him more than they would fear any boss.

"I'll be gone for a while, maybe the rest of the day," he informed her once he had his body temperature back under control.

"You don't have an out of office meeting," Sharon said.

"You're not my favorite secretary," Levi mumbled so no one other than her would catch the insult. Sharon snorted a laugh, she wasn't afraid of him.

Levi continued on to the elevator and punched the button harder than necessary. Once inside and alone, he closed his eyes and took a deep breath.

When he'd arrived in the office that morning and received the news that Angelica had called in sick he'd nearly turned around and gone to her apartment right then. He'd wanted to demand she tell him what was wrong. He'd checked on her again Saturday and Sunday night, unable to stop himself. Both times he'd watched for longer than necessary from the roof of the building next door. She'd been relaxing on the couch both times, it had seemed like her usual evening routine when home so he hadn't worried. Now he regretted holding himself back from knocking on her door to check on her more directly.

The only thing that had stopped him right then had been Sharon giving him a knowing look as he'd stood frozen in indecision. To avoid her really knowing what was going on, he'd walked to his office and slammed the door. Then he'd poured himself a drink despite it being Monday morning. He'd also texted Dalton and instructed him to stick close and to let him know if Angelica left.

Dalton had done as instructed, letting him know that Angelica left the house looking very ill and he'd driven her not to the emergency room or an urgent care clinic, but to an OBGYN. Which meant she'd thought that whatever was wrong had to do with being pregnant and that set a whole new kind of worry through him. Was there something wrong with the baby? Was she ill because of the baby? Was she confirmed pregnant?

It had taken a herculean effort to stay in his office and stare at his computer rather than march out of the office and meet her at the doctor's office. The one thing that kept him from doing that was the fact that he knew it would blow his entire cover, which he wasn't ready for. So he waited and he drank until Dalton called with a report.

Apparently she'd come out a little better though still looking ill and picking up a prescription. And she'd confirmed she was pregnant.

Levi wasn't sure what to do with the feeling that bubbled up inside of him when he read that text. Elation, hope, and terror all mixed in his body. There was no hope of getting anything done until he saw for himself that she was alright. So he was going to go to her even though he knew it was probably a bad idea, he just couldn't ignore his demon instincts.

She was pregnant with his child and he needed to be near her.

By the time he got to his car he realized he couldn't just barge into her space without a good reason. And since he couldn't tell her why he was really there—he knew she was pregnant with his kid and he wanted to make them both his—he needed an excuse. His first thought was to bring her some work, though he ruled that out mostly because he didn't want to go back upstairs and face Sharon.

What did you bring someone when they were sick? Demons didn't get colds and flus, which made them great employees. He googled it as he walked to his car.

When Levi arrived at Angelica's apartment he had a container of soup and some bottles of aloe water. He sat for an extra minute in his car to calm his nerves. He'd never been nervous to approach a woman before, and he berated himself the whole time for being such a chicken. He'd asked strangers out on dates, he'd approached women in bars, he'd even been turned down a time or two, though admittedly not very often. And still it had never made him think twice about trying again. Now he worried that he was making a mistake, had picked the wrong soup or the wrong flavor of aloe water. He worried that he was overstepping or being creepy and he wasn't even trying to date her, at least not yet. He was on the first step of courting which was trying to prove himself worthy of her time. Maybe that was the problem, he'd never tried to court anyone before. He'd very purposefully avoided anyone even thinking he was interested in a longterm relationship. What if he wasn't any good at it?

If Dalton hadn't been watching from the stoop, Levi wasn't sure what he would have done, maybe driven off. He couldn't let someone who he considered an employee see him be weak however, so he got out of his car as if he'd just been on the phone and not evaluating his worthiness.

"I assume she's still in there," Levi said as he approached the building.

"Yep, I wouldn't be surprised if she's asleep. She was looking pretty wrecked when we got back,"

"You can go. I'll let you know when you need to come back and watch the place."

Dalton nodded and walked off toward his car.

Levi frowned at the smell as he entered the building. It was musty and old, and he hated that this was what Angelica walked through every day.

As he approached her door on the second floor, his palms felt sweaty and his heart was racing. He feared her rejection even though he wasn't here to declare his intentions, he was here to give her soup because she was ill. It was a normal thing a boss might do, he assumed. He had never done anything even close to this before, maybe it wasn't normal.

Levi steeled himself against the doubts and knocked. His knuckles fell against the thin wood of her door with far too much force, the sound making him take a step back.

He didn't even have time to gather his courage to knock again before Angelica opened the door. Her eyes were wide and a sleeve of crackers was clutched in her hand. She was dressed in a tank top and shorts, a matching set she likely wore to sleep in. They were white and green checkered, and he had the sudden thought that he'd never seen anything more adorably sexy in his entire life. More of her skin was showing than he'd ever seen and his eyes roved over her trying to take it all in. His gaze snagged on a small heart tattoo on her right shoulder.

"Mr. Blackwood?"

He tore his eyes from the tattoo and met her caramel gaze. She wasn't wearing any makeup and she was still beautiful. Curls of red were falling down out of her half bun and he wanted to touch it. Wanted to tuck it behind her ear then run his fingers down her neck to her shoulder and trace that inked heart. His fingers flexed around the carton of soup reminding him why he was here.

"You're sick," he said gruffly, pushing the carton towards her.

She reached out for it. "You brought me soup?"

"And some aloe water," he said quietly, holding it up as if it excused his uninvited presence.

"Oh, thank you." She'd taken the soup he'd thrust at her but with her other hand holding the crackers, she couldn't take the bag with the waters. She looked like she wanted to say something then relented and stepped back. "Come on in. I guess you won't be surprised at how small the apartment is, since you're buying the building," she said with a nervous sort of laugh. "Welcome to my home."

He'd actually not been inside the building before because it didn't matter to him when his plan was to tear it down. He wasn't going to remind her of that at this point though.

He stepped in and took a deep breath of her air. It was cool and it smelled like her. A mix of cinnamon and vanilla that he had noticed the first time they shook hands and had never been able to get out of his mind. He didn't know if it was something she wore or if it was her toothpaste or a particular mint she liked to chew. He found it intoxicating and it was so pervasive in her home that he felt his head spin a little.

He had to give himself a small shake to focus and let his eyes drift around the space. It wasn't new to him, he'd seen it through her window almost every night for a year, but this view of it was different, so much more intimate and he wanted to growl with satisfaction. He forced himself to peruse the place as if it were all new. It was a one bedroom with an open kitchen and living area design that wasn't meant for more than a single person. A sliding glass door led out to a porch just big enough for a small bistro table with one chair. He imagined it was all plenty of space for her but he couldn't imagine even an infant fitting too. Had she expected to stay in this place after she had a baby?

His gaze continued to roam over her cluttered personal space. She wasn't dirty, there was no sign of dust or grime, it just seemed that she liked to have things around her and the lack of storage space probably didn't help. Books were piled on multiple shelves in haphazard ways and she had so many plants next to her porch door that he was surprised she could even get out to it. He knew she did, he had spotted her out there with a book and a glass of wine on multiple occasions. The couch had four blankets that he could see and as many pillows. It was drastically different from what his own sleek and minimalist style tended to be. He felt almost claustrophobic just standing there.

He was shocked to see, as he followed her to the kitchen area, that it was tidy. This part of her home hadn't been visible to him outside.

"I know I've never taken a sick day before, so maybe this isn't weird for you. I don't think bosses usually bring their secretaries soup when they call out."

"I've never had a secretary work for me for a year, so I don't really know the protocol either," he admitted.

"Well just so you know, it's not normal."

"I'm not a human, maybe it is normal for a demon."

She started to laugh and turned to face him. "I'd be less hard pressed to believe you came here to fire me in person so you could see the panic on my face at losing my job and my apartment in the same month."

"You're not fired."

"But I *am* losing my apartment, right? I suppose if I feel better later then I'll start packing. When do the bulldozers come? Or should I expect a wrecking ball?"

He could tell she was half joking but there was real worry under it too, and he wanted to ease that. "There's an empty apartment in the Blackwood building, if you want it."

"You know I can't afford that, you pay me."

"Gennie in accounting pays you." He didn't add that he would never charge her rent or that he actually wanted her in his penthouse not an empty apartment, he didn't think that was something she'd appreciate hearing at the moment.

She narrowed her eyes at him. "What is really going on Mr. Blackwood?"

He hated when she called him that and in this setting it was even worse. They were alone in her home, he wanted to hear his name on her lips. He cleared his throat before saying. "I don't want to lose a good employee because of housing issues."

She seemed to accept that answer and opened the soup container. "Oh, smells good, do you want some?"

"It's for you."

"Right, and I asked if you want some."

They'd never eaten together and it felt like a very intimate thing to do. "Okay." His entire body lit up with eagerness at what felt like an acceptance to prove himself to her. He had to tamp it down, she was human, he reminded himself, she may not fully realize what she was doing.

. . .

Angie was very confused by Levi's presence. She got out two bowls and poured the soup then handed one to him. She led him to the couch because her table was currently covered in a pile of half-folded towels. She'd get back to those later. She pushed the couch blankets to the side and motioned for him to sit.

When he sunk down on her old couch in his usual workday suit—today's was a dark blue with a light blue button up and a white tie—she nearly laughed at the odd picture it made. It didn't make her uncomfortable, this was her home and if he didn't like it, he could leave.

She burrowed into the blanket pile and turned the television back on, she'd been watching an old comfort show when he'd knocked. The soup smelled amazing and thankfully her stomach had settled a lot since that morning. She assumed in part due to the confirmation that she was experiencing pregnancy symptoms and not the flu, as well as the anti-nausea prescription.

"This is really good, where did you get it?"

"The Asian market down the street from the office."

"Oh yeah? I have tried some of their stuff but never soup. I'm not usually a soup person, it's too hot."

"Perfect for when you're feeling under the weather," he said.

She felt his eyes on her as they ate. She wondered if he was assessing whether or not she was really too sick to have gone to work. It would be a real asshole thing to do and she tried not to paint him in such a harsh light. He had delivered her soup because she wasn't feeling well, that wasn't the action of an asshole.

Sometime around the second episode of her show she fell asleep and when she woke up he was gone, the soup bowls were cleaned up, and there was a note on the kitchen counter.

Stay home tomorrow and continue to get better.

The thoughtfulness of that made her smile and a flutter of something uncomfortable unfurled in her belly. She did *not* want to start romanticizing her boss, he was a demon!

CHAPTER 9

Angie frowned down at her phone. Mike was ignoring her messages and she started to wonder if he'd blocked her. "Is there a way to tell if someone has blocked your number?" she asked Patrick as they ate lunch in the employee lounge.

"It'll say *undeliverable* or something like that when you text."

"Okay, so he's definitely getting the messages, so why isn't he responding?"

"Hot date stood you up?"

"Not exactly," she sighed and sat back in her chair.

"In the last year I've heard you mention many first dates, never a second and no complaints. So what's up with this one?" he pushed. "The dick just that good?" He wiggled his eyebrows at her.

Angie rolled her eyes then leaned forward. "Can you keep a secret?"

"Sometimes," he said with a laugh. "Depends on how juicy it is."

"Well everyone will find out eventually so," she lowered her voice to a whisper even though they were alone in the room. "I slept with a guy like a month ago and I'm trying to get ahold of him because I'm pregnant." She couldn't keep the joy out of her voice or the smile off of her face. She was still battling nausea, which was helped immensely by the prescription. Her boobs hurt to even think about, and her body temperature rivaled mount Vesuvius. And still she couldn't be happier because she was pregnant.

"I've never seen anyone so happy to be one-night stand knocked up."

She laughed. "Okay, here's the really crazy part." She took a deep breath, eager to confess the whole truth to her friend. "I went in after I got my bonus and had artificial insemination done. I was *trying* to get pregnant. It turns out I already was."

Patrick didn't even stutter, just rolled with her admission with wide eyes. "Wow, so you got the baby and the money, that's awesome." His happiness for her was genuine and Angie was glad she was sharing with him.

"Not exactly. I did the procedure as scheduled. I only found out that I was more pregnant than I should be because I went in to the doctor feeling so sick earlier this week, that's why I was home. They did an ultrasound and it turned out I was three weeks pregnant instead of two."

"So now you're out the money and have to try and contact one pump chump? Damn, girl, your luck couldn't be any worse."

Angie laughed. "It wasn't a bad lay, he just never called me again." She frowned. "Maybe it was bad for him." Ugh, that's what she had been trying very hard not to consider.

Patrick shook his head adamantly. "No way, I've seen you dance. Anyone who has moves like that with clothes on has got them with their clothes off. More like he's an idiot, as most men are. Why bother telling him if you planned to do it alone anyway?"

"I don't know, it just feels like the right thing to do, I guess. I'd want to know if I had a kid out there. I don't need him to be involved with it or me, I just need to give him the option."

"Okay, where does he work? Maybe we should just pay him a little visit."

"I don't know if that's a good idea."

"Okay then, what's his name, I'll look up his socials. Maybe he goes to the gym and we can arrange an accidental encounter. Where did you meet him in the first place?"

"I ran into him at the library actually."

"How sweet, did you both reach for the same book and sparks flew?" Patrick asked, fluttering his lashes.

"No, I dropped half the pile I was carrying and one of them landed on his foot."

"Still sounds like a *meet cute* to me. We should hang at the library and see if he shows up again."

"That could take a long time."

"If it was a true *meet cute* he would be there the next time you were."

"Unfortunately this is reality. His name is Mike Duevaux."

Patrick started typing on his phone and soon held out a picture to her. It was of Mike standing in front of the ocean wearing a pair of board shorts. His blond hair was wet and spiked and he had a big smile on his face.

"Is that a dating profile?"

"Oh yeah, I always check the dating sites first. It's actually easier to find people on there than facebook because they want to be found on a dating site."

"Okay, so he's still single, that's good I guess." Angie had held out a small hope that he'd been in a relationship or that he had entered into one immediately after their date. That would have explained why he was avoiding her so hard now.

"Should we get him to meet us somewhere then spring the baby reveal?"

"Oh god no. How about I try emailing him. That app has a messaging option, right?"

"Sure does, but you'll have to make your own account to do it.

I'm not willing to risk my dating app reputation on your baby daddy."

"Fair enough," Angie laughed. "I think I'll just text him that I'm pregnant and if he doesn't respond then that's the answer. No big deal, at least I let him know."

"Great plan. Oh, guess who I saw at the bar Friday night looking like he was having the worst time of his life?"

"Who?" Angie asked, distracted as she typed out a text to Mike that hit the right balance of serious and casual.

"Leviathan Blackwood," Patrick whispered as if the demon's full name would summon him into their midst.

Angie set her phone down and gave Patrick her full attention. "Are you sure it was him?"

"Oh yes, his brother was there too, Foras. Which isn't that surprising, the younger Blackwood is a party animal but Leviathan never sets foot in places like that as far as I've ever seen."

"Maybe he does and you've just never caught it?"

"Maybe, but he looked uncomfortable enough that I doubt cowboy vampire bars are his usual thing."

Angie's mind filled with images of Levi and sexy vampires, and she didn't like it. She'd never seen him with a date of any kind, though she assumed he had regular women he saw casually. A guy like him didn't have to try very hard for female company. Rich, handsome and with a dark power about him that drew women in like moths to a flame. No doubt they got burned regularly because the man was a perpetual bachelor.

"What's with that face?" Patrick asked.

"What face?"

"You look like you just bit into a bitter lime."

Angie wasn't sure what she was feeling and she definitely wasn't about to explain what bordered on jealousy to Patrick. "I just don't know how to phrase this text," she said as an excuse.

Patrick held out his hand for her phone and read what she'd

started. Angie tried to hold herself back from asking for any more information about Levi's wild night at the vampire bar. She knew she'd be looking for bite marks the next time she saw him.

Levi watched Angelica closely, alert for signs that she wasn't handling pregnancy well. She was more sluggish than usual and didn't look quite as bright and healthy either. He also noticed her snacking on dry crackers at her desk and drinking ginger tea. He made a point to have Sharon stock both in the lounge. He still had no plan on how or when to tell her what he'd done. Watching her fall asleep on her couch had made him yearn for more of those simple moments with her which made him want to tread very carefully through this mess. It had been nearly impossible for him to leave her there that day. He'd wanted to pick her up and take her with him, had wanted to curl around her and keep her safe. He'd wanted to do so many more things once she was feeling well enough, and now every time she was in his sight he was hard, which made things very uncomfortable for him. She didn't seem to have any clue what she was doing to him. In fact, she seemed particularly distracted today and was checking her phone way more than usual.

Regret threatened to weave its way into his mind the more that he craved her. How was she ever going to forgive him when she found out that he'd hijacked her pregnancy? If he didn't let her know soon she'd start asking questions at the next doctor's appointment because an ultrasound would reveal the fetus wasn't growing at a normal human rate. He was surprised she hadn't been alerted to it at her last appointment. Maybe they hadn't done an ultrasound, only a pregnancy test. They were likely most concerned with how she was feeling rather than the timing of her pregnancy. The doctor wouldn't be able to miss it with an ultrasound though. There was no reason to assume she'd immediately think of him as the culprit, she'd likely think it had just been a random mistake by the clinic. He doubted the witches there would cover for him even if he wanted them to, which he didn't. He wasn't planning to keep his paternity from Angelica.

He knew he had to tell her before she found out from someone else, but how? And how could he make certain that she didn't freak out and run when he did?

It had to start with a foundation of care, the same as any demon courtship that had moved into phase two. He needed her closer so he could care for her more openly. A plan started to solidify. He would wait until after he'd gotten her moved into his building, preferably his penthouse but he'd settle for the building, something he was determined to happen sooner rather than later. Which meant he needed to expedite the buying of her current building and start the process to evict everyone. Then he would prove to her that he would be a great father and mate, and she wouldn't be angry when he revealed what he'd done, she would be happy.

Even he didn't quite believe that lie.

His phone dinged, distracting him from the dark spiral he was about to slip down. When he saw who it was he didn't feel any happier. Why the hell was Mike Duevaux texting him? He was the last guy Levi had threatened away from asking Angelica out on a second date. Did the man think he could talk Levi into changing his mind?

He opened the text ready to tell the guy he was dead wrong and his vision darkened. Angelica had messaged Mike to say she needed to talk to him because she was pregnant, which meant she'd slept with him on their one date. That knowledge made Levi want to commit murder in the worst way.

His body temperature rose. His phone alerted with a message telling him that it was overheating. Levi dropped it on the desk and pushed to his feet. He paced to the window, smoke rolling off of him and his nails sharpening. He looked out at the city taking calming breaths. It was a great view but all he saw was Mike thrusting on top of Angelica and he wanted to punch something. No, not something, someone, Mike.

"Mr. Blackwood?"

Levi couldn't turn and face Angelica. If he did, he knew he was going to say something he'd regret. "What do you need?" he asked, surprised at how calm his voice came out.

"The file just arrived from accounting for the waterfront property."

"You can put it on my desk," he instructed.

"You shouldn't smoke in here," he heard her mumble as she dropped the file on his desk and walked out.

She left her scent behind and he chased it. He walked back to his desk and picked up the file she'd dropped. Her cinnamon vanilla scent was changing slightly due to the pregnancy and it had a calming effect on his anger. He managed to cool himself enough to pick up his cell and respond to Mike. He also managed to hold himself back from telling Mike to meet him for an ass beating. Instead, Levi let Mike know that no, he was not about to be a dad and to not bother contacting Angelica about it. Mike sent back an emoji to express his relief and Levi was about to change his mind about the ass-beating meetup. How could the man not be disappointed? How could he not see that Angelica was an amazing human and any man would be lucky to have her?

Levi thought about why Angelica had messaged Mike and realized that this meant the doctor must have done an ultrasound at the appointment and told her that she was further along than she should be. That could mean either it was his child, growing faster than human inside her womb, or it really was Mike's and he'd just lied to the guy, not that he felt bad about it.

Levi knew what it would mean if Angelica was pregnant by someone else. The smell of another male's offspring growing inside of her would slowly drive him insane, it was why he'd gone to the clinic in the first place. He had to know for sure one way or the other, and there was a sure way he could.

He called her into his office.

Angelica hurried in with her notebook and pen, ready to take notes on whatever he needed from her, she was so damn good at her job. Her eyes seemed to rove over his face and neck with an unusual intensity before her shoulders dropped and she gave him her usual small smile and met his eyes.

"Mr. Blackwood," she said, not sitting.

"Have a seat," he instructed.

She looked nervous but sat in the chair in front of his desk. She was wearing a simple black dress and her hair was down today, curling all around her. Levi knew he had one chance to settle his spiraling thoughts and hoped she wouldn't notice his erratic behavior. He wasn't sitting behind his desk as usual and walked to the small bar he had set up near the window. He grabbed the ice bucket as an excuse and turned to her. "I need you to set up a meeting about that waterfront property for next week and get me some more ice." He held out the bucket and she grabbed it quickly. Just as he'd known she would, she stood quickly as well. Because he was standing there to hand her the bucket, she nearly brushed against him. He inhaled. He opened all his demon senses and took her scent in deeper than he'd ever dared, letting it imprint on his soul.

"Sorry," she said as she bumped against him stepping around him and then hurried out the door.

Levi was frozen as the scent revealed the truth to him. Deep down in her scent, just budding inside of her was something he was born to recognize.

She was pregnant with his child.

She thought it was Mike's though and that meant that his hopes of holding out longer and laying a foundation were gone. She was probably freaking out thinking that she'd gotten pregnant prior to the artificial insemination and obviously wanted to let the father know. Would she be as willing to let *him* into her life when she found out it was his?

He wasn't confident that she would and he was out of time. He needed to tell her what was going on. He thought of her worried looks, her furtive glances at her phone the last few days. She'd obviously been trying to get ahold of Mike and been ignored. The stress couldn't be good for the baby and he hated for her to feel rejected. It hurt him to know that his actions were unintentionally hurting her instead of protecting her. It had been his mission since she'd walked into his office to care for her and until now he hadn't regretted a single thing he'd done with that in mind. Keeping this from her was no longer an option.

Angelica walked in his door a few minutes later with her usual smile and his ice bucket full. "Anything else I can do for you Mr. Blackwood?"

He hated that she didn't call him Levi. "Close the door and have a seat."

She looked a little surprised by his direction. "I haven't made that call yet," she explained but she did as instructed again and sat nervously in front of him. She was perfection, and he was about to turn her world upside down.

"This isn't about work."

"Oh, oh is this about my apartment building?" worry etched her brow. "Should I be expecting that wrecking ball soon?" she asked, her tone light. Her face betrayed the very real worry she was feeling.

Levi took a deep breath and ripped off the bandaid. "No, this is about you being pregnant."

Angelica's mouth dropped open, her eyes went wide, and she made a sort of strangled noise that had him leaning forward ready to provide life saving CPR if necessary.

She stiffened and closed her mouth with a snap. "How did you know? Can demons smell pregnancy hormones?"

He thought about taking the excuse, but he knew it would only make things worse in the end. He looked directly into her caramel eyes as he told her the truth. "I know because my sperm was used for the artificial insemination."

She blinked and shook her head. "No, I had a one-night stand, apparently the condom broke or something ..." she trailed off as all of what he said hit her. "Your what?" she exploded, standing up and throwing her hands out.

Levi struggled to remain seated and calm, this was his chance to start showing her that he was what she needed. He had expected this reaction of course, he knew he'd done something that she would feel was wrong. He also knew that he was going to have to convince her everything was going to be okay and that this was a good thing because he wanted to be with her and help her raise the baby.

She looked down at her empty hands with a frown then glanced around the room. She reached for a paperweight on his desk and gripped it tight. For a moment he thought she was going to throw it at him, and he wouldn't blame her if she did. She made a sound like a growl and smashed it on the ground. "Take that as my resignation," she whispered and walked out of the room.

That he had not expected and had no plan for. He was right behind her as she gathered her things at her desk. "Angelica, you're not quitting."

"Fuck you. Fuck you and this job, and your sperm! Fuck that clinic. I *am* quitting and I'm suing them, and I'm going to live just fine—" she stopped and gasped as if she were holding in tears. "I am going to be fine and so is *my* baby and you can just go fuck yourself. I can't believe you tried to steal my pregnancy."

"I didn't just try, Angelica, I did." Admitting that was the wrong thing. She whirled to him and smacked him across the face.

"I hope you're wrong because I just might murder you. And I'm definitely taking this to HR."

"Angelica, you're not thinking clearly," he said calmly as she started toward the lobby. Internally he was screaming and panicking, he couldn't let her leave, he had to stop her. If she walked out of the building right now would he ever get her back? He wanted to call security, he wanted to lock her in his bedroom.

"No, I'm not, you're right about that. You know what I am? I am *pissed,* and if you keep following me I think I might just throw something at your face instead of the floor."

He stopped at Sharon's desk and stared at Angelica as she pushed the elevator button over and over. He knew she was right and he needed to give her a little space to process what he'd told her, no matter how it went against his instincts. It nearly killed him not to stop her when the elevator doors opened and she walked in, or when she turned with head high and tears on her cheeks. He just stood there watching as she refused to look at him, just stared right through him until the doors closed between them.

That's when he lost the little control he'd had. His temperature spiked and his clothes incinerated. His body grew and shifted as he felt the loss of everything he wanted. Someone down the hall gasped and he heard footsteps running. Thankfully Sharon wasn't bothered and just shook her head at him as he walked to his private elevator. "Cancel all my meetings for today and hold all my calls," he told her. "Angelica needs to take the rest of the week off."

"You're an idiot," she said.

"I know," he grumbled and punched the button for his penthouse.

CHAPTER 10

Angie drove straight to the fertility clinic. She burst through the doors and not even their magic was enough to calm her beating heart, or her anxiety-twisted stomach. She approached the receptionist with tears stinging her eyes and hands shaking. Honestly she wasn't sure how she'd driven here safely. "I need to talk to Felicity. Now."

"Of course, why don't you have a seat and I'll let her know, what's your name?"

"Angie Walsh."

"Have a seat and I'll see if she's available."

Angie didn't want to sit or wait, she wanted answers and she wanted to let loose with the tears that were barely held back. She moved to the closest seat and sat stiffly, refusing to get comfortable because she couldn't imagine having to wait long for answers. She got a lot of curious looks from other people in the waiting room, which made her want to disappear.

She remembered being there just a few weeks ago, so full of hope and so eager to get pregnant. And she had, and she'd been so happy. She hadn't even been that disappointed to think that Mike had gotten the job done first and she'd wasted the money. But this? Had her demon boss really somehow gotten his sperm to be used on her? And if he had, did it work? She didn't know how to feel about that, and she refused to think about it until she found out for sure. Her stomach churned and she made a dash for the bathroom. She made it to a stall before unloading her stomach. It had been her least-sick day all week until now.

"My body obviously doesn't care for demon babies," she grumbled as she flushed and lurched to the sink where she rinsed her mouth and splashed water on her face.

"Everything okay?"

Angie straightened and turned to see Felicity standing in the bathroom.

"I saw you make a run for it. Morning sickness already? That's a good sign." Her voice was cheerful and she was smiling. It eased something inside of Angie.

That's when the dam broke and the flood of tears flowed. "I think we need to talk," she managed through sobs.

Felicity opened her arms, offering Angie a hug and she walked into it. She let the warmth of Felicity's body and the spicy scent of her perfume ease her through the miniature meltdown she was having. It wasn't long before Angie pulled away and wiped at her face, trying not to be embarrassed by the wet spot she'd left on Felicity's lab coat.

"Why don't you follow me to my office?" Felicity said, and held out a box of tissues.

Angie cleaned up her face then followed Felicity back through the lobby and to her office. Once seated, Angie wasn't sure if she was more angry, or upset, or some other mysterious emotion. She just knew she needed answers.

"Did you inseminate me with my boss' demon sperm?"

Felicity didn't hesitate. "Yes. He came to me that morning demanding it, and there was something the Moon Goddess saw in him that She liked." Felicity shrugged. "I don't care much for demons myself. I suppose there's something redeemable about the man if She wanted to help him out."

"What do you mean *help him out?"*

"Like I said, he barged in demanding that I use his sperm rather than the one you selected. He wanted you to have his baby."

Angie's mind spun. "Why would he do that?"

"Who knows why a demon does anything? He probably just wanted to make sure he could keep you close. He seemed like a demanding sort."

"And why exactly did you agree?" she asked through gritted teeth.

"Because of the Moon Goddess," Felicity said reverently. "I have a special connection with Her. I always do as She asks and She's never steered me wrong. Which is why I can assure you that this is not a disaster, even if the father of your child is a demon. This is good news, it will all work out, like it has before."

"You've done this before?" Why the hell hadn't she read about this in the online forums?

"Oh yes. We've aided in other artificial inseminations where the goddess has intervened and it has always worked out for the best, trust me. If the Moon Goddess said that this was the right thing, it really was."

"But I am farther along than I should be, which means I could have gotten pregnant before the insemination, this might not be his baby."

Felicity cocked her head. "Would you like me to check?"

"I think you owe me that," Angie snapped then took a breath. "Please, if you can tell me for sure, please do." She couldn't not know, she couldn't wait and see what came out in nine months.

Felicity walked around the desk. "Stand up, I just need to touch your belly and I should be able to feel if it's demon or, what did you say you slept with before the insemination."

"Human."

"Well, that will be an easy tell, human or demon." Felicity reached out when Angie stood and placed her hands on her stomach then closed her eyes.

Angie felt a tingling warmth as Felicity probed her womb with magic.

"It's demon," Felicity confirmed, pulling her hands back. "And healthy I think, so congratulations."

Angie scowled at the cheerful witch. "I want my money back. This is not what I paid for."

"Oh, I'm sorry, that's not possible. Remember, you signed the *Divine Intervention and Chaos Clause.*"

"The what?"

"It was in the contract. We can't be held responsible for the results of chaos caused by divine beings or chaos-causing entities. It's all very standard, many businesses have them these days."

"And a demon qualifies as a chaos-causing entity?"

Felicity looked thoughtful. "You know, I think it might. However, I wouldn't have gone along with his wish—like I said I am not a fan of demons—if it wasn't for the spark I felt of the Moon Goddess."

Angie felt like throwing her hands up and screaming. There was nothing more she could get from Felicity now that she had confirmation of Levi's claim. What was done was done, and obviously Felicity would never admit that she'd absolutely fucked Angie over.

"I *won't* be recommending your clinic," Angie snapped and left.

Angie sat in her car seething, something she was sure wasn't good for the baby. She tried to calm herself and think rationally. Ever since the day she'd been inseminated, Levi had been watching her differently because he had known he'd done this insane thing to her. Was he watching and waiting for her to figure it out? What did he expect to happen now?

She had no answers, couldn't even fathom what had made him decide to impregnate her when he had never so much as looked at her with desire. Obviously this pregnancy had nothing to do with a relationship, otherwise he would have asked her out at some point. So did he just think she had good DNA and wanted a half-demon baby with her? If that was the case, why hadn't he brought it up? She wasn't sure what she would have said to him if he had. It was insane, sure, but also she wanted a baby and she'd think twice about denying someone else a baby.

So many questions and no answers. What was she supposed to do now?

She was pregnant, she was alone, she was about to lose her apartment, and she'd just quit her job. She had no one to turn to for help in this town, not really. She could probably stay with Patrick or Sharon for a week or two. She couldn't expect them to support her through a job search if it took longer than that, and certainly not a baby too. There was only one very responsible party in this whole mess, and there was no reason he should just go on like nothing was wrong. No reason he should be able to hit up vampire bars on the weekend like he was any other bachelor looking for a good time. If he wanted her to have his baby, he would deal with the consequences. Something tugged at her brain, some assurance that she was on the right track no matter how ridiculous it was, so she started shoving clothes in suitcases.

Levi was brooding in his penthouse, staring out at the darkening city with a drink in his hand. He hadn't gone back into the office after letting his emotions get out of control. Instead, he'd spent the second half of the day going over every possible scenario and hating most of them. Angelica could already be on her way out of the city. That thought had him stalking around his penthouse in full demon form until Dalton texted to say she'd arrived home looking upset and hadn't left again. But his thoughts continued to bombard him with scenarios that made him want to burst into flames, she could have terminated the pregnancy. He didn't think she'd ever forgive him for putting her through that and he wouldn't blame her. The worst thought of all was that she could be sitting in her apartment alone and crying. That's the thought that had him pouring a drink. She was suffering and it was his fault when all he wanted to do was care for her. He drank and stared out at the city as he waited for the sun to set so he could fly to her and see for himself that she was okay, and it was one of the longest waits of his life.

He normally loved to look out his windows and imagine the things he'd be a part of creating in the city. Tonight, all he could think about was what he'd tried to create with Angie and if he'd ever get to know the result.

He wasn't an idiot, he knew it had been a rash decision and he knew it had been sneaky and, well, very demon-like. He couldn't change what he'd done, and he didn't want to. He just wanted a chance to prove to Angelica that he was a good choice for her and the baby. He tried to reason with himself in case Dalton reported that she'd packed a bag and headed to the airport. He'd have to let her go, he'd have to respect her wishes, and yet he knew he couldn't. He'd chase her down, he'd follow her across the world. And it didn't even matter if she wasn't pregnant still, he would do anything to make her his, something he should have admitted after the first time they met.

He was about to go to her, the sun was set just enough for him to fly unseen but a knock at his door stopped him. There were very few people who knew the code for his elevator and were able to come knock on his door directly. Everyone else had to buzz in from the lobby. Dread that it was his brother filled him as he crossed the room. He didn't have the energy to deal with Foras' idea of helping him out of a slump.

When Levi opened the door and found Dalton standing there with a pile of suitcases, he didn't know what to think.

"You've got baby mama drama," Dalton said and just then the elevator doors opened behind him. Out walked Angelica with more bags draping her body and clutched in her hands.

"Angelica?"

"You stole my uterus, you are about to kick me out of my apartment, and you made me quit my job. The only good idea I could come up with that didn't make my stomach ache was to move in with you, asshole."

She shoved past him and Dalton gave him a sympathetic look. "She needed help."

"Thanks, bring it in." Levi grabbed some bags and Dalton got the rest. "Just set it there, I'll figure it out."

"Good luck," Dalton said, then lifted a hand at Angelica who was walking around as if she were inspecting a rental. "See you around, Angie. If you need anything, call me. I put my card in one of the bags."

Levi didn't like that, and he sent a glare to Dalton, letting fire flash in his eyes. He was impressed by the young man's shrug.

"I've got her car keys, I'll bring it over and leave them downstairs. She was way too upset to drive and I didn't want her lugging all this stuff around by herself. She's a good person," Dalton said and walked out.

"Yeah, she is," Levi whispered as he shut the door.

Levi turned to find Angelica standing there with her arms crossed, glaring at him. "I haven't evicted anyone yet. I haven't even officially purchased the building, so don't you think you're overreacting?" He regretted the word choice as soon as it was out of his mouth. He wanted to reach out and pull the words back but he was helpless to do anything other than watch her perfect face twist into a scowl that was somehow adorable.

"Isn't this your plan?" she snapped, pointing at him for emphasis. "And you get whatever you want, don't you? So why put it off? I don't have a job so I can't pay rent anyway."

"You have a job," he said with a heavy sigh and shot back the rest of what was in his glass.

"You smoke in here?" she demanded, ignoring his comment.

"No."

She looked like she didn't believe him. "It's bad for the baby so you'll have to stop. Where's my room?"

Levi ran a hand down his face and tried to cool his body. She was trying to make him angry, he knew that. He didn't have to let it work. What was worse was that she was here, in his space and yes, this was exactly what he had wanted. This was a huge win in the demon mating handbook and would usually mean he'd won against other suitors, that she'd chosen him. His body reacted as if he were about to lead her right to his bed even though he knew that was the farthest thing from her mind right now.

"I'm glad you're here," he said.

"Don't smoke in the house anymore, I can smell it all over you," she sneered.

"That's just the way I smell," he huffed, not willing to explain the details of demon emotional reactions to her right then.

CHAPTER 11

It was him. Levi naturally smelled like sweet smoke and the realization intrigued Angie more than she would have liked. She'd always loved the smell that seemed to roll off of him from time to time. And she'd told herself that it was a sign of a very bad habit on his part in order to keep some distance between them. If it was just his natural scent, that changed things. She swept her gaze over him as he stood there as if she could pinpoint where the scent emanated from. Embarrassed at her perusal, she focused back on his face. He had a bland look that she didn't believe. She knew that look. It was the one he wore when he really wanted a deal to go through and didn't want anyone else in the meeting to know how badly he did. It worked well in an office setting with people unfamiliar with him. It set the other party on edge and made them feel like he couldn't care less so there was no reason to try and make the deal better for themselves. His stoicism in this moment was belied by his hair which looked like he'd been running his hands through it before she'd arrived, and his unbuttoned collar, loose tie, and pushed up sleeves. He looked more bedroom than boardroom and it made her lower body tingle with an eager warmth.

Shit, she did not want to lust after him while she was mad at him. "Where should I put my things?" she asked, trying to keep her mind out of the gutter. She wasn't sure why she was here except every other idea she'd come up with had made her anxiety spike and her stomach twist in knots. She didn't need to make any more rash and possibly terrible decisions tonight.

"This way," he said, his voice low. She'd never heard him use that voice before. It was so sensual she shivered. Thankfully he'd already turned so he didn't witness her embarrass herself.

Angie followed Levi past his living room, which was pristine, and frankly, dreary. It was everything she'd expect from the man. The furniture was all hard lines and modern designs. Nothing looked comfortable, or babyproof. There was a lot of glass and sharp edges, and even the black leather couch looked like it would hurt to sit on. They went past a very clean and modern kitchen she doubted he actually used, then down a hallway that didn't have a single thing hung on the dark gray walls.

He stopped at a door and motioned her in. "This is where you can stay. It has an attached bathroom so you should be comfortable. My room is further down the hall. There is also an office and a reading room farther down. I don't expect you'll need to go in my office or bedroom, but anything else is open for your use."

"And I would have expected you to stay out of my womb," she said and pushed past him into the bedroom. It was a guestroom meant to be universally pleasing which meant it had nothing pleasing about it. White everywhere with a few accents of green and gold. The bed did look comfortable and she was exhausted so she planned to use it soon. With the stress of the day and the pregnancy hormones, she was sure she could sleep for twelve hours straight.

Other than the bed, there was a dresser in a light wood that matched the nightstands. That was it, no other furniture in the room and the couple of paintings hanging on the walls looked like they came with the comforter set. "Who decorated this?" she mumbled.

"Decorator, same as most of the rest of the house."

"That makes sense."

Levi frowned. "I'll grab the rest of your bags." He turned and walked back down the hall.

Angie explored the rest of the room. There was an open door leading to the bathroom, it was dark inside so she couldn't tell if it was equally plain as she expected it would be. She opened another, smaller door and found a closet to hang a few clothes in. When she pushed aside the curtain beside the bed she gasped. It wasn't a window, it was a door leading out to a Juliet balcony. She hated that she liked even one part of this room but she did, this was amazing.

"I forgot that was there," Levi said when he came back in the room. "My brother is the only one who's ever used this room and I don't think he even moved the curtains, he tends to sleep most of the day away."

Angie had never met Levi's infamous brother but rumors of his antics flew around the office. "I hope the sheets have been washed."

"Yes, it's clean," he assured her.

Angie nodded, she'd have to take his word for it. "It's cool for now, although I'll need more space when the baby comes," she said, dismissing him. Angie walked into the bathroom and shut the door, then waited until she heard the bedroom door close.

She slumped against the sink and looked around the brightly-lit room. It was a standard bathroom with a tub and shower. The towels were white and the hand soap dispenser was gold. There was a white and gold rug on the floor. The only thing missing were green accents to match the bedroom. It was the type of bathroom she'd expect to find in a nice hotel with absolutely no personal touches. She washed her hands and splashed some water on her face then left the bathroom. She swept her gaze around the bedroom just to be sure Levi hadn't stuck around.

She sighed when she saw it was empty and looked at the bed. She was tired, she was also hungry. She'd been so angry with Levi that she hadn't stopped to eat dinner before packing her belongings. When she'd lugged the first suitcase outside her apartment building she'd run into Dalton who just shook his head and offered to help. He hadn't seemed surprised that she was coming here. She hadn't even had to give him directions which made her suspicious. When he'd hit a code on the private elevator that would take them to Levi's penthouse, she'd glared at him until he admitted that he was sort of employed by Levi. Though he had refused to tell her what exactly his job description was, she had a feeling she knew.

Dalton had shown up after her first day of work for Levi. Why did Levi hire someone to watch her?

No, that was too ridiculous, it had to be a coincidence. Maybe he'd hired Dalton to watch the building and let him know when the right time to swoop in and buy it was? Somehow that seemed even more far-fetched.

Either way it was not something a normal person would do. A normal person would also not have gone to a fertility clinic and demanded his sperm be used to inseminate his secretary. There was nothing normal about Leviathan Blackwood.

She huffed and decided that she definitely did not want to see him again tonight so she took her toiletry bag into the bathroom and started a bath. Maybe tomorrow she'd demand some answers.

When she left the bathroom, clean and relaxed but still hungry, she smelled something mouthwatering. It was tempting enough to get her out of the bedroom despite her desire to ignore Levi until after she'd gotten some sleep. Honestly she wasn't sure she would be ready to see him tomorrow either, though it seemed more likely.

She walked to the bedroom door and cracked it. Damn, whatever he had ordered smelled good. Her stomach started to make ungodly noises at the idea of food, so she gave in and slipped on some loose sweats and a soft T-shirt with a tiger on it. Then she left the bedroom.

The scent of garlic and onions wafted down the hall mixed with the tang of tomato. Surprisingly she heard the distinct sounds of cooking. He hadn't ordered something, he was making pasta, she loved pasta. Did he know that? Was this a trick to get her to forgive him? She tiptoed down the hall and spied him in the kitchen pulling a loaf of french bread out of the oven and she thought maybe it was a really good way to gain her forgiveness.

"Are you hungry?" he asked without turning around.

The crunch of the bread as he sliced it had her biting back a moan. She had to clear her throat before speaking. "I could eat," she said, then her stomach growled again. "I didn't know you cooked."

He chuckled as he turned with two plates piled with pasta drenched in tomato sauce and sliced bread. "I cook. I hope you like Italian."

"It's okay," she lied with a shrug and took a plate from him, then went to sit at the table. Like everything else in his home, the table was without embellishment. Just a slab of crystal clear glass held up by gray metal posts. Seriously not babyproof.

Levi joined her, sitting across the table. She didn't want to encourage conversation and he looked like he'd like to ask her something so she started eating, eyes on her food. It was as delicious as the smell had promised and in no time she was nearly done and feeling wonderfully full.

"Oh my god, pregnancy eating is no joke," she groaned to herself, forgetting that she wasn't actually alone just because she was refusing to acknowledge Levi.

"Have you had any unusual cravings?"

She glared at him across the table. "I'm going to bed, gotta rest up for job searching tomorrow."

"Angelica," Levi said, his voice thick with exasperation. "You are not quitting your job."

"Why? Because if I work for someone else they might try to trick me into having their baby?" she snapped. "Fool me once," she snarled.

"You can take tomorrow off if you need it, I know that this is all a lot to think about."

"Do you? Do you think it was *a lot* to replace the sperm I was supposed to be inseminated with? Was this a well thought out plan Levi? Did you have Dalton following me to my appointments at the fertility clinic? Going through my garbage to find the hormone injection needles?"

"I didn't—no it wasn't thought out. I had my reasons," he gritted and stood, taking her plate to the sink.

"Don't care what they are," she said cheerily and walked to her bedroom with no intention of setting an alarm.

CHAPTER 12

Levi cleaned the kitchen with a vengeance. Angelica was in his home and she'd eaten his food. She was sleeping in his guest bed tonight. He concentrated on those things and ignored the tightness in his gut over her accusations. She had every right to hate him. His demon instincts were to provide, to prove he was a male worth keeping. She was giving him that chance, if unintentionally.

A week later she hadn't given him many more opportunities to prove himself. She'd refused to come to work and he'd refused to accept her resignation which meant there was no hiring a new secretary and Sharon was getting overworked. Angelica *had* eaten three meals a day that he cooked, he was even coming up at lunchtime. She thanked him politely each time but never offered more. She ignored his questions about pregnancy and only told him about jobs she'd found listed online. Each mention of sending off her resume made him want to throw her over his shoulder and set her down at her desk.

"I hope they don't call me for a reference because I'll tell them you're still employed," he responded between clenched teeth each time. Then she'd get up in a huff and slam her bedroom door and he'd clean up the meal feeling like he was failing harder and harder every day. Maybe he wasn't a good mate, but then why would she be here? Except she wasn't a demon female and she had no idea that by moving into his home she'd accepted his courtship. He couldn't balance the two ideas and it was driving him crazy. He walked around his house smelling her and his cock was constantly hard, he stared at her empty desk and growled at his employees. He was lucky they didn't quit on him. He'd even lost a deal with the waterfront property because he hadn't been able to keep his temper under control when the investor had asked where his sweet secretary was. If she were a demon he would think she was testing him, but she was a human and he had no idea what she thought she was doing.

Her pregnancy was very obviously progressing and that gave him a selfish satisfaction. Her breasts, already having been large and luscious, were huge now and her body temperature was closer to his own, which was convenient since he tended to keep the temperature in the penthouse around sixty. He heard her puking daily even though she was taking medication to help with the nausea and she ate the snacks he made sure to leave in the kitchen for her. Soon she'd need new clothes to fit a growing belly and of course all the baby items.

He realized how massively unprepared he was for a baby in his penthouse. Perhaps that was what was making her so unwilling to settle in, he hadn't provided a nest, at least not a good one. A demon male was supposed to provide the perfect environment for a family. He had seen the distaste on Angelica's face when she'd first walked into his penthouse, how had he not realized this sooner?

When he tried to bring it up to her she'd snapped something about moving to Montana and then he'd had to leave the room because his suit had started to smoke. He couldn't let her leave him.

He wasn't sure what else to do and he was running

dangerously thin on patience so he did something he really didn't want to do, he approached Sharon.

"You have children." Maybe it wasn't the best way to start a conversation, but he was far too frustrated to beat around the bush.

"Three," Sharon agreed.

"And your husband is full demon?"

"You've met Greg."

"How long did it take for you to choose him, when did you know he was going to be a worthy mate and father?"

Sharon's face went soft and she smiled wistfully. "I felt the attraction immediately, but he is full demon so I knew that if I didn't make him work for it he would never take me seriously. I didn't want him for a night or two, I could feel a tug on something deep, something that must come from my demon DNA because it had never happened before and I'd had long term boyfriends who I felt some kind of love for. I made him work for me for a couple months before I told him that I wanted him as my mate and for him to father my children."

"A couple months," Levi frowned at that, they didn't have a couple months before the baby was here. "Right. Okay, so I need you to talk to Angelica."

She raised an eyebrow at him. "And try to convince her to come back because you can't find a better secretary? You know I can't make her want you, right."

"No, that's not what I'm asking you to do. Can you come up to my place?" Levi didn't want to try and explain everything in the office where anyone could overhear.

Sharon's eyes widened. "You have her in your apartment? Is she there willingly?" Sharon whispered.

"Of course willingly, what the hell kind of demon do you think I am?"

"I've worked for you a long time Leviathan Blackwood, and I've never seen you act the way you have since the day Angie walked in this building. She changed something in you and you've been moving around her like a coiled snake ever since. I may not know what you've done, but I am surprised it took a year for you to spring, honestly."

Levi didn't like the woman's accurate assessment, however her demon understanding of the situation was one reason he wanted her to go talk with Angelica.

They went upstairs in silence. Levi had never invited any employees to his home and he felt suddenly weird about it. It wasn't that he disliked them all, he actually considered Sharon a … well not a friend, a friendly employee. Maybe he should have hosted some get-together in his home at some point, except then he'd have people he really didn't care for in his personal space and that didn't seem like a good trade.

"Wow," Sharon said when they walked in his front door.

"What?"

"It's exactly what I would have expected from you."

He wasn't sure how to take that, so he ignored it. "Angelica," he called out. He knew she was here, he had security cameras throughout the building and parking garage so he would have seen her leave.

When she didn't answer his shout he directed Sharon to have a seat in the living room and went down the hall to find her. She wasn't in her room, the door was open and a quick look showed it was empty. He continued on to the only other room he ever found her in.

She was there, curled up on the small couch in his reading room, asleep with a book still clutched in her hands. She'd had wide eyes and even gasped a bit when he'd shown her this room. It was the one space in his home that had a cozy vibe, according to her. He tried to pretend he didn't understand, but he did. It was wall to wall bookshelves, stuffed beyond capacity so there were piles in places too. The furniture was dark and rich because it had come out of his father's office. Everything else in the penthouse had been picked from a book his designer had shoved in front of him, and he had given little thought to any of it aside from his bedroom.

There was something about this room becoming her favorite that made his heart squeeze. Maybe he could provide an acceptable home for her if he put his mind to it. He left her there to rest and went back to Sharon in the living room.

"She's napping and I don't want to wake her. She doesn't sleep well at night."

"Are you going to tell me what's going on?"

"She's pregnant, and it's mine."

"Wow, I didn't think she was the type to sleep with her boss."

"She's not," he said quickly, wanting to defend her from office gossip. "She went in for artificial insemination and they used my sperm."

"I'm guessing that was by your design?"

He grinned at her, "Well, I *am* a demon."

"So she's having a half-demon baby and I'm guessing she's pissed about it?"

He nodded.

"Wow, and how did you manage to get her to come live with you?"

"I offered and she took me up on it." It wasn't the whole truth and he could see the doubt in Sharon's eyes. He didn't elaborate.

Sharon nodded and smiled slyly. "Interesting."

"What's interesting?" Angelica asked, walking into the room looking adorably sleep rumpled.

"You being here," Sharon said.

"Where else would I go? Levi is the cause of my current problems, and he should pay for it."

Levi couldn't deny it, and he didn't want her anywhere else, so he said nothing.

"Why are you here?" she asked Sharon with a smile. "I've missed seeing you every day."

"Everyone has been missing you this week too." Sharon stood and hugged Angelica.

Levi had a spark of jealousy at the sight. Angelica had never been that happy to see him.

"Levi thought maybe you'd want to talk to someone with experience in demon pregnancies." Sharon explained and sat back down.

Angelica glared at Levi and guilt made his body heat. "I explained the situation to Sharon," Levi defended. "I know you are friends, so I didn't think you'd mind."

"You have no right to announce my pregnancy to anyone," Angelica snapped at him.

Levi's body heated further and he saw Sharon lean away from him. He had to calm down. The last thing he wanted to do right now was flame up or start to shift form in front of Angelica.

"He's worried about you," Sharon said. "You know he wouldn't have willingly revealed what an idiotic thing he'd done if he wasn't desperate. Come sit. Levi, make yourself useful and get us some herbal tea. Peppermint or ginger would be good for Angie's stomach."

"He is an idiot," was all Angelica said then sat down.

Levi didn't want to leave, he wanted to monitor what was said between these two. He also knew that Angelica wouldn't open up like he thought she should if he watched. So he forced himself to go make them tea and then he went back downstairs to work. Which he knew would actually only consist of him staring at his computer and wondering what the hell they were talking about.

CHAPTER 13

Once Levi was out of the penthouse Angie sighed with relief. "I am still not sure why I'm here," Angie said honestly.

"I think you were probably correct earlier when you said you wanted to make Levi pay for what he did. You know you have options, right?"

"I know, and I thought about it for a minute when I found out, trust me. There are a lot of reasons that I'm going through with this pregnancy, and I am, I want this baby so much it hurts," she admitted and tears stung her eyes.

"Well, it makes sense that you're here then, because if you're pregnant with Levi's baby then you'll want to be near him. It's hormonal."

Angie didn't respond right away, just sipped her tea and thought about that. She'd started to feel that way in the last week. When he was out of the penthouse she was anxious, and when he was home she was annoyed at him for what he'd done to her, but the anxiety was gone.

"Is it a demon thing?" Angie finally asked.

"Sort of, yeah. What you need to understand about demons is that the males are the subordinate gender when it comes to matings and family planning. A female will make suitors vie for her attention and compete against each other to prove that they are the best provider. When she chooses one and allows him to impregnate her it is because she's found him worthy of her and able to provide for her and the child or children. Once pregnant, if there wasn't already a loving bond between the two, then one usually forms. I assure you there isn't always a bond from the start aside from sexual attraction, and in some cases a real love bond doesn't even form after the baby is born. Picking the best provider doesn't come with automatic love. The woman will want to be near the father during pregnancy because of the hormones, and she will crave the touch and attention of the man. This usually continues after the baby is born. My mother and father couldn't hold it together after I was born, but my husband and I grew closer with each pregnancy." Sharon shrugged.

"Great, so this fetus is making me desire Levi?"

"His company at least. Not sexually I don't think. Sexual attraction generally comes before the courting, so it isn't really an issue. And sexual attraction doesn't automatically lead to a courting for demons. Haven't you ever been sexually attracted to a guy you wouldn't want to let put a baby in you?"

Why did Angie's mind have to conjure a picture of Levi at that statement? "Um, yeah I guess so."

"Right, so you're not going to suddenly want to fuck him because of the hormones, that's not their intent. They just make you want to be near the father of the baby so he can keep you safe until it's born. Survival instincts, you know?"

"That's not why I moved in. I had to quit my job, because he is an asshole, and he's going to evict everyone in my building. So where else was I going to go?"

"I'm not saying it was hormone-driven, I'm just letting you know a bit about demon physiology."

They sat in silence for a while, both sipping tea with their own thoughts. "Is he really concerned about me?" Angie finally asked. "Or is he just missing his secretary?"

"Both? He is definitely worried that you're not handling the news well and probably regretting his heavy-handed method of trying to keep you. We both know he hates when I have to be his secretary."

"Heavy-handed," Angie huffed. "More like slick-handed." An image of Levi's hand wrapped around his cock as he stroked himself into a cup filled her mind and her body flushed with arousal.

"Gross," Sharon laughed as if she were reading Angie's dirty mind.

"It doesn't explain why he did it," she said with a shake of her head.

"If I had to guess, I'd say he was afraid of losing you."

"Why the fuck would he think that? I need that job. I'm pregnant, I need money and insurance."

"Demons don't exactly think reasonably when they want something," Sharon said softly.

"If he wanted a baby he could have asked, or found someone willing. Jesus, the man is rich and sexy as hell, a million women would have been happy to let him get them pregnant."

"You really think it was the baby he wanted," she said with a laugh. "Hun, you are delusional if you think that man isn't head over heels for you."

"Me? No he—" Angie stopped when she saw the serious look on Sharon's face. Did Levi want her? He wanted to keep her enough that he'd assured his sperm was used to impregnate her. It was insane and it was devious and it was ... well it was demon-like. She should be pissed and she should be running for the hills. Truth be told she was more than a little flattered and confused. "Why didn't he ever hit on me in the last year if he was so interested?"

"Who knows, probably some kind of weird rule he had set for

himself. No sleeping with his employees or some shit. Maybe he just didn't want to lose a good secretary."

Angie shook her head. The possibilities were endless and only one person could answer those questions. Sharon *could* answer other pressing questions that Angie had. "Okay, forget Levi. What am I in for with this pregnancy?"

"It'll go fast. Half-demon pregnancies are about six months. When it's born everything will be normal. You won't even really know a difference until puberty, then it might develop an overheating problem."

"Overheating? Like fevers?"

"Not exactly. Demons have a tendency to burst into flames when they get really upset. So they have to learn control fast before they become a danger to those around them. Usually it only takes a couple months, sometimes longer. If the child starts to have those signs, Levi will be able to help guide her through it all."

That explained a lot, and proved she wasn't going crazy, she really had seen smoke coming off of Levi a time or two. "Okay, I guess I'll deal with that when it happens."

"And it might not. Half-demons are only fifty percent likely to develop that particular issue."

"Good to know. So other than feeling attached to Levi while I'm pregnant and a shortened gestation, I have nothing to worry about?" At least she knew why she'd felt so drawn to move in with him.

"Nothing at all."

The relief Angie felt was consuming and she slumped against the couch. "I suppose I'll have to talk to Levi about why he felt this was necessary."

Sharon shrugged. "He deserves to suffer for his actions, don't be too quick to forgive him. He literally trapped you into having his baby. Don't go easy on him."

Angie could tell there was more Sharon wanted to say so she waited.

"He's also a really nice guy. I've worked for him for a long time and I have seen him be an absolute shark in business and a bit of a bear to work for. I've never seen him be cruel. Talk to him, make him tell you his reasons. This couldn't have come out of nowhere."

"Thank you Sharon, I really appreciate your input."

Sharon pulled her in for a brief hug. "Any time, hun. I am just downstairs if you need anything or you can call me whenever. Even if you just need to vent about what an asshole Levi is."

Angie laughed and hugged her back. It was so nice having a friend.

Sharon left and a few minutes later Levi was back. Angie was waiting, and she had questions.

"You've had me watched since I started working for you. Why?" She decided to start with something easy.

"You live in an unsafe neighborhood."

She couldn't deny that truth. "What else have you done behind my back?" He looked uncomfortable with that question and she crossed her arms over her chest, which she then dropped because damn, her boobs hurt. She settled for hands on her hips. "If you lie to me, I am packing my things and I am leaving. I will go to Montana and stay with my sister, I swear Levi, I won't stand here and be lied to or manipulated." She could feel heat radiate off of him and the sweet smell she'd grown to love filled her nostrils.

"I have discouraged the terrible choices in men you've dated from asking you out on a second date. I was only watching out for you, they weren't worthy, obviously. If they were then they wouldn't have been so easily deterred."

Angie's mouth dropped open. "You're the reason—you—oh my god, that wasn't your choice to make. That was such an inappropriate thing for an employer to do." The relief at knowing she wasn't undateable was almost enough to stifle the anger over his admission.

"Maybe it was," he said. She didn't think he believed it.

She remembered what Sharon had said about demon biology. "Is this some kind of weird demon thing?"

"Probably," he admitted.

"Are you aware that being pregnant with your child makes me want to be near you?"

His eyes widened in shock.

"You didn't know that?" How could he not have known?

"I can't say I'm sorry, but I swear, I would never use this pregnancy or the feelings it may invoke to get you into my bed."

She believed him. His face was creased with concern and his voice trembled with fear.

"Apparently it's not a sex thing, just a presence thing," she clarified.

"Oh, so is that why you moved in here?"

She wasn't sure, so she didn't answer that. It was time for the big question. "Why did you have me inseminated with your sperm?"

Levi ran a hand over his face and into his hair. "I knew that I couldn't handle you smelling like another man. I would have gone crazy knowing another had claimed you, even in such an impersonal way as artificial insemination. I wouldn't have been able to work with you every day knowing that I'd lost."

"Lost what? Damnit Levi my uterus is not a competition."

"I know."

"Do you?"

He just pursed his lips.

"Right, well your freaky demon ideas have ruined my life."

"No, they haven't," he said softly.

"Maybe not, but I don't forgive you."

"You don't have to."

"And I am not sure how long I'll stay here with you. It isn't baby-friendly."

Levi looked around. "That can be fixed. I'm not attached to any of this."

"I need a job and I don't have the energy to search any more." She hadn't done much searching despite what she'd told him. It had been too depressing. There were only a couple jobs that paid well *and* she was qualified for, and they had both been out of the city. "So I'm coming back to work and you're giving me a generous raise."

"Okay."

Angie hated when he was so agreeable. How was she supposed to be mad at him if he just gave in to everything she demanded? "I'm going to take a nap."

"I'll have dinner for you when you wake up."

Angie walked to her room without another word and laid on her bed. She grabbed her phone and wasn't at all surprised to see a text from Patrick.

Sharon went upstairs with Levi. Why aren't you here to gossip with? I miss you, I hope you're alright.

I am fine, lots going on. I'll be back at work soon. And no, before you even start to spiral, Sharon and Levi are not having an affair, I can vouch for that...

I want to believe you but it's more fun to imagine they are. This place is boring without you! Come back soon.

I'll see you Monday.

YAY!

Angie missed her friends at work and the idea of going back to her routine made her happy. Sitting around the last week ruminating on the disaster of her life and what her future might hold had been a bad idea. Of course, that's exactly what her sister had told her when she'd called her the first day here. She'd wanted Angie to come to her immediately and that hadn't felt right either. So she'd waited, hoping she'd wake up from this bad dream.

After talking to Sharon she wasn't sure it was a nightmare, maybe it was just a twisted fairy tale. Maybe she was about to get a happily ever after with a morally gray hero who had a body that made her mouth water and a scent that made her legs wobble.

That line of thinking had her reaching for her vibrator.

CHAPTER 14

Levi looked around the apartment and frowned, then he made a phone call.

"Leviathan, do you miss me already? I can be in town in an hour and we can go out," Foras said when he answered.

"How do I make a place safe for an infant?"

"Are you planning to steal an infant?"

"Shut up, you know Angelica is pregnant with my child."

"So you're planning to steal a pregnant woman."

"Just tell me."

Foras sighed heavily. "Infants don't need things around them to be safe. Toddlers however, put everything in their mouths and they fall constantly. Your place is a death trap for a toddler."

Levi knew Foras was right, he was going to need to make major changes in order to prove he was going to be a good father.

"Have you told Mother?" Foras asked slyly.

"No."

"Are you going to?"

"Obviously."

"Before it's born?"

Levi just grunted and hung up. He had no intention of

introducing Angelica to any of his family before he had a solid place in her life. He could see the disdain on his mother's face if he introduced Angelica as his secretary who also lived with him and was pregnant with his child. Anything less than fiancée pregnant with his child would be unacceptable, and for once he agreed with his mother. He wanted everything with Angelica, and now that they were communicating, he thought he could get it. He sat down with his laptop and started doing some research. Before long, the sun was setting and he hurried to make dinner.

When Angelica emerged from the bedroom she looked fresher than she had all week. She'd showered and had her hair loose. It curled wildly around her face, which was finally free of the dark circles and worry lines. She was wearing a casual summer dress that reached the floor in a tie-dye pattern in all shades of purple. He'd noticed early on that she wore a lot of purple.

"I hope you're hungry, I made pork chops and steamed vegetables with rice."

"It smells amazing. Everything you make is always good, I had no idea you could cook."

He shrugged at the compliment even though his heart fluttered at her praise. She'd eaten his cooking constantly in the last week, but she'd never said much about it. "I like to cook, it relaxes me after stressful days."

She sat at the table and he served her.

"What else do you do to relax? I know you work out, and I now know you read and cook."

He nearly smiled at her questions. Usually they ate in silence or he talked and she frowned. This was a step in the right direction, and he was afraid of making any sudden movements. He sat down and served himself before answering. "That's about it. I'm not much of a television guy. I like a movie here and there, no sports. I like whiskey, as you know. That's my biggest vice. What about you?" He craved personal information about her.

Even having Dalton watch over her, he hadn't ever invaded her privacy in any way so there were still so many things for him to discover.

Like the taste of her, his mind purred and suddenly his pants were tight.

"I like television, mostly comedies and stuff I've watched a million times, it's comforting. I like to crochet while I watch, keeping my hands busy. I like reading too and wine, though that's out for a while now. I enjoy going out and dancing, but again, that is not something I'll be doing for a while. My ex, Grayson, and I used to hike a lot, it was really more his thing than mine. I like being outside especially when the sun shines, though I don't want to exercise in the sun, I want to meander."

Levi had never asked about her previous marriage. He'd known about it of course, it was in her background check. The most interesting thing he'd seen was that she'd never taken his last name in all the years they'd been married. He wanted to probe for more information about the man who had been stupid enough to lose her, but he wasn't sure she was ready for that.

"Hiking has never appealed to me either. I prefer my outside adventures to include water and sand."

"Beach time! Yes, I like to go to the beach at least once a month and just soak up the sun and smell the salty air. I think that's still okay when I'm pregnant," she added with a frown. "I'll have to check with the doctor at my next visit."

"When is your appointment?"

"It wasn't supposed to be for a few weeks, because this was supposed to be a normal pregnancy." She sent him a look across the table that was more annoyed than angry and he thought that was a vast improvement.

"And now?"

"Now I need to see if they even take on half-demon pregnancies and then see how that changes my appointment schedule."

"I would like to go with you," he said, then held himself stiff, ready for her rejection.

She set her fork down and took a drink of water. He couldn't breathe as he waited for her answer.

"What is your end goal here, Levi?"

God he loved when she called him Levi instead of Mr. Blackwood. It was like a caress and every time she did it he wanted to close his eyes and indulge in fantasies of her saying it while he pleasured her. And his pants tightened even more.

He moved uncomfortably, trying to ease the pressure. "I want to be a father to your baby."

She nodded. There was something in her eyes that didn't match the movement, that didn't seem satisfied with his answer. Did he dare hope she wanted more?

"Great, okay. Well then, I guess you can do father stuff like come to appointments and hear the heartbeat and all that." She took a big breath and let it out slowly. "What are we going to tell people at work?"

"Why do we have to tell them anything?" He'd never shared personal things with his employees, until today with Sharon of course.

Angelica looked at him like he'd just said the stupidest thing possible. Maybe he had. "I won't be able to hide this pregnancy very long, especially with the increased growth rate. Would you like me to tell them that it's an anonymous donor, or that you tricked me into having your baby?"

Neither, he wanted her to tell them that she was his and he was hers and that they were creating a life together. "Why not tell them that we are having a baby together and leave it at that."

She rolled her eyes. "Oh yeah, that works great for the big bad boss. I'll be inundated with questions and not only that, they'll all assume I seduced you or trapped you with getting pregnant. They'll probably think we've been fucking for the last year and that is the only reason I stayed working for you. Oh god, they are going to hate me."

Levi watched in horror as she burst into tears. She sobbed into her napkin and he didn't know what to do. He knew what he wanted to do; pick her up and comfort her. He didn't think she'd go for that though. He couldn't even deny her worries, this was a delicate situation, for her in particular, and it was his fault she was in it. It presented him with a chance to help her, and prove that he was worthy of her and the child she was creating.

"Let's get married," he said impulsively.

She froze, all sounds of crying stopped, then she sniffed and dropped the napkin. And started laughing. She laughed and laughed for so long and so hard there were tears in her eyes again for a different reason and she was grabbing at her stomach with gasps by the end.

Levi felt his body heat with embarrassment and anger as he watched her reject him with so much enjoyment.

When she was finally calm, he gritted out, "What is so funny about that? It makes sense and it would solve the issue with the other employees."

"No it wouldn't," she laughed, wiping her eyes. "They would call me a gold-digger and they would say I trapped you and you only married me because you got me pregnant. Levi, I don't know how you don't see the problems with that ridiculous suggestion. Not to mention, then we'd be married and I don't really want to look forward to a second divorce in my future as soon as you feel like having a real relationship with someone compatible."

He bared his teeth at her because her suggestion that he'd want anyone else was ridiculous. "Fine, what do you suggest?"

She looked thoughtful.

"I think we should say that we had a one-night stand and we are having a baby together, but we aren't together. It's close to the truth without revealing too much. One drunk night, no big deal, and I'm staying with you so you can help me save money while I'm pregnant in order to move into a place big enough for me and the baby."

"No."

"No?"

"No, I have never slept with an employee, they'll never buy it." He actually had no idea if they would or not, he just didn't want her to put something like that between them, another barrier he'd have to cross.

"Well, I'm not marrying you just so you don't look like a womanizer."

"Then why don't we tell them that we've been dating for a while and that we had a surprise pregnancy so now we are trying to see where it goes?" It was a compromise he hoped she could agree to, because the last thing he wanted was for her to remain appearing single.

"I guess I can agree to that. Can you really pretend to be dating me? I don't think I've ever seen you with a girlfriend. I assume you date often, casually. I will have to ask that you not see anyone else while you're pretending to date me. I obviously won't be dating for a while."

He almost told her that he hadn't dated anyone even casually since she started working for him. He didn't think she'd believe it. "Of course, I would never embarrass you like that."

"Thank you," she said and he saw her whole body relax. "Okay, I think it will work alright and we can figure out the breakup later when it makes sense. Something amicable of course, you won't have to be the asshole or anything."

Smoke filled Levi's nostrils and he had to work hard to keep from completely combusting at her words.

"Are you okay?"

"Yeah," he managed as he wrestled control of his body from his emotions.

CHAPTER 15

Angie ate the rest of her dinner, which was very good as usual, alone. Levi had started to smoke, she'd caught the scent of it and he'd looked red in the face, angry. But why? At first she'd thought he wanted an end date for their fake dating. When she'd tried to suggest it he'd gotten even smokier and left the room. Now she was alone with her thoughts and doubts.

None of this was her doing, so if he didn't like some part of it then that was on him, he'd put them in this situation. He was lucky she wasn't making it harder, and she thought he should really appreciate that.

After she cleaned up and retreated to her room she called her sister.

"So you're living with, and fake dating, your boss who got you pregnant not by accident but by design and subterfuge? This is like next level romcom material. You should sell your life story to the highest bidder."

Angie did not appreciate her sister's levity. "I am trapped in a situation where I am having my boss' baby and living with him and continuing to work with him. So to make things smoother we will let everyone think we have been dating for a while."

"I think that's what I said."

Angie wanted to growl at her sister. "This is not what I called you for."

"Why don't you just come live with us, Angie, seriously. I don't think this situation, as amusing as it might be on paper, is a good thing. I think you are setting yourself up to be taken advantage of."

"I'm living with him rent free."

"You're having his baby for free. Has he told you if he plans to support it or you after it comes? Did he pay you back for the insane amount you spent on artificial insemination? What about doctor visits and the birth? Will he be paying for any of that? Is there going to be a parenting plan in place?"

"Stop!" Angie shouted into the phone, tears in her eyes. "I don't know, okay, I don't know any of that." Her emotions had been wild today, she couldn't believe she'd broken down in tears in front of Levi, with her sister it was more understandable.

Henley took a deep breath. "Angie, girl, you need to think things through and you need to think fast. Apparently you don't have nine months to figure this out. I just want you to be safe, and I want you to be happy."

"I'm safe, for now," she assured her sister. She wasn't sure how long that might be true, and it wasn't as if any of her sister's questions weren't valid. It was just that Angie hadn't thought about them and when she did, she started to panic.

There was a soft knock at her door.

"I have to go. I'll call you in a couple of days."

"Stay safe and think about what I said."

"I will."

They hung up and the knock came again, this time with a question. "Angie, I heard you yell, are you okay?"

Angie opened the door and found Levi standing there looking worried.

"I was on the phone with my sister."

"Why were you yelling at your sister?"

"You have siblings, don't you sometimes disagree?"

"Yes, I have disagreed with my younger brother, Foras a time or two."

"I'm the younger and like you, my sister thinks she knows what's best for me."

"I don't—"

"Yes, you do, otherwise I wouldn't be here in this situation, would I?"

He pressed his lips together. "So what does your sister think is best for you?"

"Moving in with her in Montana." Angie watched his face closely when she said those words. She saw his eyes flare and his jaw clench. "I am not ready to make that decision yet." His whole body relaxed. Was he really afraid of her leaving? Did he want to be a dad that badly?

"Would you like some ice cream?"

All other thoughts and worries left her at the offer. "I'd love it. I don't think you have any though." She knew he didn't because she'd seen everything in his kitchen over the last few days. It was all very healthy and annoying.

"I can order some delivered along with whatever else you might want. I realize I hadn't asked what kinds of foods you might want stocked, and since you aren't moving out any time soon, we should fix that."

She smiled at him. "I'll make a list."

That statement seemed to please him and he quickly pulled out his phone. He opened the shopping app before handing it to her. "Just add anything you want and then hit deliver."

Angie walked to the couch with Levi's phone in her hand and started adding everything she'd been craving or missing since she hadn't been in her apartment.

An hour later it was all delivered and they settled in front of the television with peppermint ice cream and peach pie. She felt spoiled and she loved it, even as she told herself not to get used to it, this wasn't a permanent situation.

The next day Angie was surprised by Dalton showing up with a few boxes of things from her apartment and telling her that everything else that he didn't think she'd need right away was in a storage space in Levi's building. She wasn't sure how to feel about Levi moving her completely out of her apartment without asking. Then again, she had moved into his penthouse without asking so maybe it was fair.

"He's given everyone a three-month warning on closing down the building and told them that they will all get their deposits back next month so they can use it to move into a new place," Dalton explained when she asked if everyone else was being evicted this weekend too.

"Wow, that seems generous."

Dalton just shrugged. "Mr. Blackwood isn't a bad guy. The city knows he's a hard-ass in business, but he isn't unfair."

Angie wasn't sure if that was right or not, she hadn't lived in the city long enough to know his reputation beyond the people who worked for him. They would definitely describe him as a hard-ass.

"I hope he paid you to do all that work for me."

Dalton winked at her. "He did."

When Angie confronted Levi about the way he was handling the evictions he just said that it was what he always did when planning to do a teardown rebuild.

"Is Dalton out of a job now that I'm living here and don't need to be guarded?"

"Dalton has many talents and I have offered him a job on the crew that will be razing your old building."

Angie was happy to hear it, and surprised that Levi would care enough to do that. Then she realized that nearly every employee at his business that she'd come across in the last year had worked there before her. Aside from his apparent inability to keep a secretary, he kept employees hired and happy without issue. She was disappointed in herself for being so surprised. Hadn't she always thought that he wasn't so hard to work for as his past secretaries apparently thought.

She pulled out her phone and texted Sharon.

Why do you think Levi was unable to keep a secretary ever?

It's a little late to background check on the job.

I just mean that he has no trouble keeping employees anywhere else in his business, only secretaries?

If you ask him he'll say he's too demanding and they were all too sensitive.

And if I asked you?

I'd say he didn't want to be that close to a woman day in and day out that he wasn't interested in, it isn't the demon way. Proximity equals intent. I didn't consider it before, since they were human, but it makes sense.

Angie wasn't sure how to respond to that so she didn't. Had Levi been after her since she started working for him? That seemed ridiculous, though it would explain why he hadn't been terrible and why he had scared off her dates. So why the hell hadn't he ever said anything to her, why not just ask her out if he was interested?

On Sunday there was a furniture delivery. Five men came into the penthouse and removed the sharp-edged tables and chairs and even the uncomfortable couch. Then they brought in warm wood tables with rounded corners and a couch in a lavender that almost passed for gray and was as soft as butter. Angie sunk into it as soon as the movers left and immediately fell asleep.

If Levi made the place any more comfortable she might never leave.

On Monday, Angie got ready for work. This would be the first day in the office pretending to be dating Levi. How did you dress for fake dating your boss? She wanted to look extra professional and extra modest. She also felt bloated so that narrowed it down quite a bit. She settled on a loosely fitted black dress with a purple paisley print around the hem and a high neckline. It made her feel good in her changing body. She slipped on some black flats and a lavender cardigan, then smoothed her hair with a little curl cream and put on her usual modest makeup. When she stood in front of the mirror she decided she looked normal and not at all like she had seduced her boss and trapped him into a relationship by getting pregnant.

When she walked out of the bedroom, Levi was standing in the hall looking as sexy as always in a dark suit and gray tie. His hair was styled back and his intense eyes drifted from her head to her toes and back to her face. He cleared his throat, "Ready?"

"Oh, yeah I suppose we can go down together. We may as well start pretending to be in a relationship before I start looking pregnant." She tried to keep her tone light but she could hear the nerves there so she was sure he did too.

His gaze whipped down to her stomach and back up. His lips tightened and he gave a short nod. Once in the elevator she started to panic. There would be no going back after this, not easily at least.

"Last chance to change your mind," she said as the elevator stopped and her heart pounded. She wiped her sweaty palms on her dress and bit her lip.

"That happened a long time ago," he mumbled and grabbed her hand as the doors opened.

Then Angie stepped out of Levi's private elevator with her hand in his and walked through the lobby of Blackwood Construction in front of at least a dozen employees who would spread the news like wildfire through the whole company. By noon everyone would know that Angelica Walsh was sleeping with Leviathan Blackwood. They would say horrid things about her and when they found out she was pregnant it would only get worse. She could hear it now. *Slut, tramp, gold-digger.*

"I think I'm going to be sick," she said, and ran for the bathroom.

CHAPTER 16

Levi's joy at walking into the office with a claiming hold on Angie's hand had quickly turned to concern as she bolted for the bathroom looking pale. He froze in indecision. He wanted to go to her and help her through whatever this was. He also was all too aware of the fact that they weren't in a real relationship so she might not appreciate him witnessing whatever was going on in there.

"Maybe I should have let her quit," he mumbled to himself.

"She's just nervous, can you blame her?" Sharon whispered. "I'll go check on her," she added louder.

Levi was thankful and continued on to his office. He sat behind his desk and turned on his computer like usual. He didn't notice what was on the screen, all he could do was listen intently for the sound of Angelica's footsteps. He needed to know that she was okay.

When she finally arrived with a weak smile and his coffee in her hand, he let out a breath of relief.

"You don't have to do that."

"What?"

"Fetch my coffee."

"Oh yeah, and what is it you'd like me to do?" she challenged. The mood swing was fierce and he felt like apologizing, if only he could figure out what he needed to apologize for.

"I just mean if you need to rest, you can go back up to the penthouse."

"I don't need to rest, I need to get all this over with."

"Get what over with?"

"Facing the whole company thinking I'm sleeping with the boss."

It finally sunk in then what was going on. "I'll have a conversation with them, no one will treat you different."

"Oh sure, that won't make things worse. Do me a favor Mr. Blackwood—"

"Don't call me that," he seethed. She'd started to call him Levi since she moved herself into his penthouse and he refused to let her go back.

"Fine, Levi, do me a favor and just don't get involved, okay? If you start treating me different then it will make things worse. We are supposed to have been dating a while, right? Just treat me as usual to prove to them that I'm not getting special treatment because I'm sucking your cock."

She turned and walked away after that statement, leaving him with a sudden and raging erection.

He got no work done that day. Instead, he spent it entirely engrossed in watching everything that Angelica did and how she seemed to be feeling. He watched as she sipped tea and snacked on crackers. It seemed like that combination helped her stomach settle and color return to her face. He noticed what had to be an unusually large number of employees stop by her desk to chat throughout the morning. All of them sent a curious look through his open office door and he had to quickly pretend to be engrossed in whatever he could. None of the interactions seemed hostile and at no point did Angelica seem upset. However, his anxiety never settled because he couldn't be sure. He didn't want to upset her again by asking, so he was forced to just watch and wait for a sign that she needed to be rescued.

When it was time for lunch she got up and he expected to see her walk to the lounge, but she stood in his doorway instead.

"Do you want to come upstairs for lunch? I forgot to pack something this morning and I know you usually go up or order in. You haven't told me to order in yet."

Eating had been the farthest thing from his mind all morning. "We have some leftovers from last night," he said and stood. He didn't grab her hand as they walked to the elevator together. It didn't feel necessary, and although he wanted to initiate the contact with her, he knew she didn't want it the same way. She did walk closer to him than she normally would, more like they were a couple and he enjoyed it. As soon as the elevator doors closed them in she stepped away, creating a space between them that felt massive.

It was all pretend for her, but every moment felt more and more real to him.

After a surprisingly pleasant lunch in Levi's penthouse, Angie didn't want to go back to work. She dragged her feet to the elevator not because she was tired and missed the afternoon naps she'd gotten last week, but because everyone down there was looking at her like they'd discovered her deep dark secret. Worst of all, they didn't look surprised.

What about her screamed, *I sleep with my boss,* so much that they weren't shocked by the revelation that they were dating?

"What's wrong, are you feeling ill?" Levi asked as they rode the elevator down to the office level. "Did you take your anti-nausea pill this morning?"

"I took it." She breathed deeply before continuing. "I knew that it would be weird to fake date you in front of everyone, I just didn't expect them to be so judgy about it."

Levi frowned at her. "Who said something rude?"

"No one is *saying* anything, that's the problem. They are all looking at me like they aren't surprised I'm sleeping with you. I thought they thought more of me, that's all." She shrugged, it didn't really matter, they were coworkers. Maybe she'd thought they were friends, apparently not.

"I'll talk to them."

"No! Oh god no, that would make it so much worse. We just have to let it all blow over. When it's old news it'll be fine again." Until they found out she was pregnant, then the gold-digger talk would start up all over.

When they got off the elevator Levi once again held her hand then dropped it at Sharon's desk and motioned for her to continue on. When Angie reached her own desk area she found Patrick propped against her desk with his eyes glued to his phone screen. They lifted to hers when she approached, and they were wide with shock. His lips lifted and he crossed his arms over his chest.

"Why the hell did I have to find out about this from Sam in marketing? I thought we were friends! And then I thought you were going to spill to me at lunch, but you didn't show up. What the hell? I need all the details."

Angie searched his face for judgment. All she saw there was curiosity, excitement, and a little hurt. Relief filled her. Here was a friend, a real friend. She opened her mouth to tell the lie and froze. If this was a friend, he didn't deserve to be lied to.

"Listen, it's not all it looks like. I'll tell you everything I swear. Not now though, let's meet after work?"

He agreed eagerly and walked away, passing Levi as he went. "Mr. Blackwood," Patrick said with a smirk.

"Good afternoon, Patrick," Levi said stiffly.

The rest of the day passed like normal except that she could hear Sharon questioning anyone's motive who tried to get past her desk to come in Angie's direction. No doubt Levi had told her to run interference. Angie appreciated the thought and also wondered if it was only going to make things worse. The best thing to do would be to act completely normal and let the curiosity burn out fast. Not having to answer more stupid questions with leading looks however, that was very nice.

"Ready to go home?" Levi asked at the end of the day. There was an eager look on his face, as if he couldn't wait for this awkward day to end as well.

"Actually, I'm going to grab a coffee with Patrick. Well, tea," she said, one hand touching her stomach.

He stiffened. "Oh, I see. Will you be home for dinner?"

Was that disappointment in his eyes before he covered it? And *home*? That word didn't fit how she felt about his penthouse no matter that he'd made some very comfortable changes with her in mind.

"I don't know," she said and stood, then reached for her purse. This wasn't a real relationship and she didn't want to start feeling like she had to answer to him about her free time.

"You'll need this then," he said and pulled out a black card. She recognized it as the same one he used to access the private elevator as well as his front door.

"Oh, won't you need this to get up there?"

He cleared his throat. "That one's yours. I meant to give it to you last week but you didn't seem eager to leave the penthouse." He shrugged as if he weren't giving her a key to his home. Which shouldn't be significant because she'd already moved her ass in there. It felt big though, it felt more permanent than him getting new furniture.

"I can just call you when I'm done."

"What if I'm not home?"

That struck Angie in a way that was very uncomfortable. She

shouldn't care where he was going, they weren't in a relationship. They had agreed not to date anyone but what did that really mean? Would he not go out and try to get laid? How could she ask him not to?

"Great," Angie snapped and grabbed the card, then hurried away. Thankfully Patrick was waiting in the lobby because she could feel Levi following closely behind her and she did not want to talk to him anymore.

"Ready?" Patrick asked excitedly and cast a look over her shoulder at Levi. "Is Mr. Blackwood joining us?"

"Nope," she said sharply and jabbed at the elevator button. She felt heat pouring off of Levi as he passed her and leaned down to kiss her cheek.

"See you later," he said and went to his elevator as if he hadn't just sent a shockwave of desire down her spine with that simple and quite chaste kiss.

Angie couldn't speak, she couldn't even look at Levi as she waited for the elevator doors to open. He'd only done it to keep up appearances, she knew that. Her body however, thought it was a greenlight to orgasms.

Both elevators opened at the same time and Angie couldn't stop herself from glancing over at Levi as she stepped in. He stood outside of his, the door open and waiting for him. His dark eyes tracked her with a dangerous edge that sent a thrill up her spine. When the elevator doors closed her away from him she took a steadying breath.

"Wow. If a guy looked at me like that, I think I would follow him anywhere," Patrick said.

"We aren't dating, I'm pregnant." She spewed the truth because she could not handle any talk of what Levi's look might have meant, not while her knees were weak and her thighs were clenching.

"Pregnant?" Patrick stuttered, all conversation ended when the elevator doors opened on another floor and people flooded in. Levi rented out space on a few different floors to other businesses and even a few apartments. He was really very smart and she'd always thought highly of him as far as his business sense goes. She supposed she could hope that their baby got his business savvy. The thought brought a slightly hysterical giggle out of her mouth and she slammed her hand over it as Patrick looked at her with wide eyes.

It wasn't until they were seated in a cozy coffee and tea shop that Angie laid out the entire story.

Patrick stared at her with shock for so long that Angie finally kicked him under the table. "Say something."

"I think you need to get away from him. You should definitely go live with your sister in Montana."

"Ha, ha, what do you really think?"

"I think he's a psychopath, Angie. He forced his way into your womb via witchy nurse and some supposed goddess?"

"It wasn't—okay it was exactly like that. I just don't feel like it was harmful, am I crazy?"

"Yes," Patrick said without hesitation.

"He's really been wonderful ever since he told me."

"He bought your building so you'd be forced to move in with him."

"He bought it because it's a good investment and he's giving the tenants a really great deal. It'll help them improve their living conditions."

Patrick just shook his head. "Okay, so you obviously are in love with him."

"What?" She reeled back in her chair and her tea sloshed, splashing her leg. Thankfully it wasn't too hot. Angie frowned and put the cup down then grabbed a napkin. "I think you might be the insane one here," she accused.

"Why else would you be excusing his predatory behavior? This feels like one of those situations where you end up dead or in a basement."

"She shook her head. I'm in his guest room and he's taking very good care of me. I am seeing how it goes, nothing permanent has been decided."

"Except sharing a child with him for the rest of your life."

"Except for that," she agreed because judging by Levi's actions, he wanted to be a part of the baby's life. She'd never deny him a presence in his child's life, even though it had come about in such an unexpected way. "And because honestly it feels good to not be alone right now," she admitted. "It feels good to have the father of this baby with me while I go through all the pregnancy things."

"And it must feel good when he looks at you like he wants to devour you," Patrick leaned in to whisper.

Angie shivered, thinking about the look Levi had given her when she'd gotten into the elevator. It had been possessive and consuming. She had no answer that she was willing to give Patrick or admit to herself.

They finished their tea and discussed baby names, then Patrick walked her back to the office. When Angie swiped the card to access the private elevator she started to get nervous. Levi had been home every evening since she'd shown up on his doorstep. What if he was out tonight? She had only been with Patrick for a little over an hour, but it was plenty of time for Levi to have changed and gone to meet someone.

Or invite someone to come to him.

What if she opened the door and found him tangled on the new couch with some woman?

Anger filled her and underneath was a hurt she tried to ignore. Tears filled her eyes and her hands fisted. She was ready to act like she didn't care and maybe never speak to him again. When she opened the door she smelled tomato sauce and fresh bread just like that first time he'd cooked for her and the knife twisted in her heart.

It was worse than she'd thought, he had made dinner for someone else. That felt like more of a betrayal than him just fucking someone. She wished like hell that she didn't have to pass through the dining area to get to her room where she could lock herself away and cry in the bathtub.

She couldn't hear any conversation coming from the kitchen so she had some hope that they were somewhere else for the moment and she could slip through unnoticed. She tiptoed toward the kitchen and saw Levi's back. He was dressed in a pair of lounge pants and a T-shirt. It was the most casual she had ever seen him. This looked intimate, this looked like something he'd throw on after *being* intimate … oh god he'd already fucked the woman and now he was making her dinner.

Angie stepped back, ready to bolt back out of the penthouse. She'd go out for dinner and stay gone for a few hours then come back. Hopefully by then Levi would once again be alone.

Unfortunately she forgot what was behind her and she knocked right into a small table holding a glass bowl that slid right off and shattered on the floor.

Levi jumped at the sound and hurried out of the kitchen. "Angelica, don't move there's glass everywhere."

"It's fine, it's fine, I'll just clean it up and get out of the way." She knelt down and reached out without looking. She grabbed a jagged piece of glass and sliced her palm. "Fuck," she cried and pulled her hand to her chest.

Levi rushed to her side and grabbed her wrist to inspect the wound.

Angie waited for his date to appear and witness what a disaster she was. "It's fine, I'll just go get a bandage. I'll be out of your hair."

Levi ignored her and continued looking at the wound. "I don't think there's any glass in it. It is bleeding a lot." He tore off his shirt and pressed it to her palm.

Angie was distracted by the sight of his bare chest. She'd known he would be muscular because he worked out. She hadn't expected the huge tattoo that covered his pecs. It was some sort of bird surrounded by flames and it was beautiful. Its tail trailed down his abs and her eyes followed it right to the start of dark hair leading even further down to disappear into the waistband of his cotton lounge pants.

Her mouth watered at thoughts of what was just a little farther down.

CHAPTER 17

Levi felt her gaze like a stroke of her finger and his cock stirred urging him to grab her and kiss her. Her hiss of pain broke the moment and he pulled her to stand instead. "Let's clean this up." His voice was low and gruff and he hoped she didn't notice the bulge in his pants, what kind of asshole got turned on when his woman was cut and bleeding?

"I can do it," she insisted and her eyes darted around the kitchen and dining room as he led her to the sink.

"Are you looking for an escape? I don't drink blood you know."

"I know, I just thought … never mind what I thought. Dinner smells good," she said quietly as he rinsed her hand under cool water.

"I had hoped you'd make it back in time, it's about ready."

"Thank you," she said quietly.

He looked up from her hand to meet her eyes. They were caramel pools of emotion he didn't understand. He hoped it meant she was seeing him for what he was, a caretaker and a capable partner, rather than what she feared he was, an asshole and a manipulator.

"I'm sorry today was hard," he said, knowing it hadn't gone great even if it hadn't felt like a disaster to him.

She shrugged. "I'm sorry I broke your bowl."

He looked over at the glass on the ground. He wouldn't tell her that the thing had cost more than she made in a year, it didn't matter. "It wasn't my favorite glass bowl," he said with a smirk. "Hold some pressure on that, I will get a butterfly bandage. I don't think you need stitches but it's deep."

He bandaged her hand, cleaned up the glass, then served her dinner. And the entire time he was hiding his elation at this chance to take care of her in another way. She was very quiet during the entire ordeal until about halfway through the meal.

"I don't think we should sleep around while we're fake dating," she said.

He was caught off guard, a bite almost to his mouth. He froze and stared at her. Then he connected a couple of dots and smiled.

"You were jealous."

"No I wasn't."

"You were running away, you thought I had some hottie in here when you got home."

"This isn't my home."

"Yes, it is," he said firmly and had to act quickly to calm his heartbeat and cool his temperature. "This is your home now and I already told you I wouldn't date anyone while we are dating and that includes sexual relationships. I didn't think I needed to be specific."

"Good," she said shortly and went back to her dinner, avoiding looking at him.

The knowledge that she'd cared made his heart swell. That she'd been distracted and jealous at the thought of him with another woman gave him hope. No matter what she tried to project, she was starting to care about him too. All he had to do was capitalize on that spark and make her start to see him as a desirable partner. As he looked at her across the table he felt something he'd never felt before and he knew that his heart was vulnerable to this woman. She was perfect and he wanted to be perfect for her.

The rest of the week went about as awkward as Monday had. The majority of Angie's coworkers watched her with smirks and whispers after she passed. She knew what they were saying and she also knew there was nothing she could do about it. She didn't want to sic Levi on them so she didn't complain, just went about her workday as if nothing had changed except that she arrived and left on the same elevator as Levi. At least Sharon and Patrick knew the truth so she could count on them for support when she started to freak out about the whole situation. They also ran interference and shot down drama talk when they heard it. By the end of the week, interest had waned among most everyone. She was sure that was partly because there was never any more PDA than hand holding. She thought it showed a level of maturity in their relationship that proved it was more than a fling between a boss and his secretary.

Unfortunately, it was the weekend of the company anniversary party and that meant she was attending the party as Levi's date. She wasn't sure they would get away with only hand holding at an event like that.

"Did you bring a date last year?" Angie asked Levi as they rode the elevator after a half day of work. Everyone got off early so they could get ready for the celebration.

"Did you not attend last year? You were working for me."

"No, last year my sister had flown down that weekend to make sure I was settling okay. So I didn't go. I'd just started working for you anyway so I didn't know everyone, it would have been awkward."

"Well then, no I didn't bring a date last year. I don't think I've ever brought a date, actually."

"Wow, hard to find someone who enjoys your sunny company for a free dinner?" Angie couldn't help teasing. She had been his secretary for a year and never had a woman come to visit him socially or called without a business reason. She didn't think he was celibate, he was way too hot and wealthy for that. She did wonder if it was a choice on his part, to remain single, or if there was something more going on. Maybe he didn't show anyone else the parts of himself that she'd just started to see which would make relationships hard to keep.

"I don't enjoy company most of the time," he said.

She didn't buy it as an excuse, but she also didn't feel like she had earned a right to his deep dark secrets. So she asked something she thought would be easy. "When's the last time you had a serious girlfriend?"

He looked uncomfortable at her question, his eyes locked on the elevator doors. "I wouldn't say I've ever had a serious girlfriend, demons don't date seriously, they court who they want when they are ready for a commitment. But the last girlfriend I had was a year ago."

The elevator doors opened and he hurried out, leaving her behind to mull over the significance behind that statement, and why it made her so happy. She knew she probably had a sly grin on her face as she walked through the door to the penthouse he held open. His own mouth was set in a grim line.

Had he just revealed something to her? She dared to hope, dared to think that perhaps this beautiful and moody man had been attracted to her from day one. Not only that, but he had held her against every other woman he encountered in the last year and found them wanting, not her. Not that he was courting her for a serious relationship, she reminded herself. He just … well he just thought she'd make a good mother to his child she supposed. Was that all it was? And why did that thought hurt so much?

Angie stood in front of her closet an hour later and frowned.

She had already started to notice changes in her body, and many of the things she'd normally pull out for an event like this just didn't seem like a good choice. Too tight around the stomach or chest, or both. She pulled out a long black dress with a modest neckline and a slit up one leg. It wasn't dressy but it was forgiving fabric. She would add some jewelry and heels and it would work. The party was only for employees and their spouses so there wasn't an expectation of ball gowns.

When she walked out of her room she found Levi looking devastating in a tux and she felt like the ugly stepsister he was being forced to go to prom with.

"Maybe I shouldn't go," she said as she watched Levi's eyes take her in from head to toe. She'd put her hair up in a twist and added some sparkly clips, as well as a diamond necklace and matching earrings. It didn't feel like enough to be on his arm, he looked so perfect.

"You look amazing, Angelica."

"None of my dressier dresses fit quite right anymore," she grumbled and smoothed her hands down her expanding figure. "This is all I feel comfortable in, it's not really a party dress."

Levi frowned and nodded. "You think you're not dressed up enough but all I see is a beautiful woman." He took off his tie and jacket, then unbuttoned the top of his shirt. He had suspenders under the jacket she hadn't noticed and when he rolled his sleeves up slightly and waited for her opinion, she had to bite her lip. He looked even more amazing like this. He looked like he was about to take her to bed instead of to a party and she was far too intrigued by that idea for her own good.

His eyes flared as if he were reading her mind.

"We should go," she squeaked out.

"Angelica—"

"It's fine," she cut him off from whatever he was about to say. The fiery look in his eyes promised passion and she didn't think she was strong enough to say no. "I'll be fine in this, and you look ... good too."

He grunted but offered her his arm, which she took. His muscles under the thin fabric of his shirt were hot and hard. She felt her panties dampen. When had she become such a horn dog? It had to be the pregnancy hormones. She looked at him from the corner of her eye, her gaze snagging at the triangle of exposed skin of his chest and she swallowed. Maybe it wasn't just hormones, maybe it was him. She'd always been attracted to him of course, he was sexy as hell. She'd never considered anything because he was her boss and she'd never date someone she worked for. The power dynamic would be too skewed. Somehow the idea of being under his control didn't sound so bad anymore. In fact, if he wanted to push her up against the wall right now she thought she'd melt.

"Angelica, are you okay? You're breathing hard and your cheeks are flushed."

Levi's words sent mortification through her, cooling her libido, and she pulled away from his arm to push the elevator button. "Great, just anxious about this gathering. We have to make sure they think we're a couple."

"So we'll dance and talk, it will be fine."

Dance! He wanted to dance with her? That would involve a lot of touching, a lot of closeness.

"Perhaps we should have discussed this before, I thought it was obvious," Levi said and she realized she must have made some kind of noise that he took as disagreement.

Angie cleared her throat, "No, of course we'll dance. It is what people who are dating do."

"Great," he said simply and they walked into the elevator.

The party was being held at a nearby hotel and even though it was a short drive, Levi had hired a towncar for the occasion. Angie didn't know what to think when the driver in a suit held a door open for her and nodded at Levi. She'd never been treated to such an experience before. She supposed it made sense, if Levi wanted to drink at the event then he wouldn't want to drive home after, although she could have.

"If you didn't want to drive you should have let me, you didn't need to spend all this money," she said as she settled in the back of the luxury car, as far from him as she could manage.

Levi shook his head. "We are supposed to be enjoying ourselves tonight, not worrying about driving or parking," he said.

She supposed she couldn't argue with that. Levi was in a completely different tax bracket than she'd ever been in.

When the car stopped she reached for the handle.

Levi stopped her. "Wait, Angelica. Frasier will open my door and I will assist you out."

"Right, fake dating rules. I almost forgot." That was a lie, she couldn't stop thinking about it on the drive. What would she be expected to do as his fake date at this party? Dance with him and stay close, she hoped that was all. She couldn't imagine a scenario where it would be expected that they kiss, that wasn't a work party expectation surely and Levi didn't strike her as the PDA type. That didn't mean she could stop thinking about it. She was far too curious about his taste, she imagined it would mimic his intoxicating smell.

Angie waited as instructed and the driver, apparently his name was Frasier, opened Levi's door. Levi stepped out, then leaned in to assist her. Angie slid across the seat and grasped Levi's hand. His palm was warm and his fingers were strong as they wrapped around hers. She felt a little silly, it wasn't as if she really needed help getting out of a car. She couldn't deny that it made her feel special, as if she were a celebrity. There were no paparazzi or screaming fans waiting to greet them though, just a doorman and he had a big smile for them and a friendly greeting as they entered the hotel.

Levi slipped his hand around her back when they were

through the door and settled it at her hip, keeping her possessively close as they walked. Angie had to bite her cheek to keep from shivering at the move.

"Relax," he whispered in her ear, "you're as stiff as a board."

If she relaxed, she was sure a moan would slip from her lips. "I'll try," she whispered back tightly.

There were a few coworkers with their significant others standing around when they walked into the lobby and half the chatter stopped as they all turned to stare. Angie imagined they were all thinking what an incongruous couple they made. No matter that Levi had done what he could to look more casual, he was still stunning and she was rather ordinary despite her jewelry.

Her instinct was to pull away from him and get the eyes off of her. He must have felt her try because he tightened his hold. She didn't want to make a scene so she stayed where she was, her face heating with embarrassment. Levi moved her forward through the lobby, his grip never loosening. He greeted everyone, both employees and spouses as he headed toward the ballroom which was just opening up for their group.

"You know everyone's name," she whispered.

He looked at her with a slight frown. "Of course I do, why wouldn't I?"

"Trust me, most company owners don't know all their employees, let alone their employees' spouses." Her last employer hadn't even known she was married apparently since when she told him she was quitting because she got divorced he had looked like he didn't believe her.

"Welcome, Mr. Blackwood. I hope you find everything to your liking," a man who must have been in charge of the hotel events said as they entered the ballroom.

Levi made a show of looking around before answering. It was a typical hotel space with white walls and floors. The tables that were set up around the outside of a dance floor all held beautiful purple bouquets and linens in a lilac. The color choice surprised her, she would have guessed black or gray. There was a bar and some waiters already standing around with trays of food as well as what looked like a salad bar, and a band just getting set up. It was amazing. Angie knew how much it had cost, she'd seen the invoices come in. He didn't skimp on this event, but it still surprised her to see it and know that his employees would have been happy with half as much. That just wasn't Levi's style she was starting to realize, he gave everything to his company and that included his employees.

She looked at him as he finished his own visual inspection of the room. He was not what he appeared to be and maybe everyone in the company had already known that. He was kind and generous. He was also demanding and shrewd, which when you were on the other side of a business deal meant your feelings about him were not positive.

"Perfect as always, Carl, thank you," Levi finally said.

Carl beamed and Angie caught sight of some sharp teeth, he was a vampire. Levi shook his hand and Angie didn't miss how Carl's hand slipped briefly into a pocket after the shake. Levi was a smooth tipper, how long had he had that in his palm?

"Angie, you look lovely," Sharon said, hurrying over with her husband who was a very tall and balding man with rich brown skin and kind eyes. "Have you met my husband, Greg?"

"Of course, great to see you again, Greg."

They shook hands and Angie relaxed at the ease of this interaction, not an ounce of judgment in Greg's face, although he probably knew the whole sordid truth. They quickly slipped into a conversation about his business. He owned a small plant nursery and Angie had a love for houseplants. Levi shifted anxiously beside her.

She gave him a stern look. "You don't have to be next to me all night, that's not what dates do," she hissed. "Especially when we both know all of these people."

"I'll keep her safe," Greg said with a nod at Levi.

Levi nodded back stiffly and squeezed her hip before moving to speak with Gennie and her wife, Lucy. Angie relaxed now, with Levi's imposing presence at a safer distance and started to really enjoy herself. It wasn't difficult, she considered many of these people friends. She was hit with the realization that she didn't want to lose this, not these people or her job. She hoped that whatever happened with her and Levi, it didn't ruin this for her.

CHAPTER 18

Levi didn't like leaving Angelica's side. Having his arm around her and presenting her as his, settled some kind of base instinct in him that he wasn't exactly proud of. Walking away from her felt like he was leaving something valuable out on the street for anyone to come by and snatch. At least he'd left her with Greg, a married demon he respected.

"I can see the rumors are true," Lucy said with a smirk.

"What rumors?"

"You've gotten yourself involved with your secretary and I'd say you're involved deep since you can't stop looking her way," she teased.

Her words made him imagine going deep with Angelica and his cock reacted approvingly. Levi cleared his throat and forced his gaze to stay on the two women he was talking to instead of straying back to Angelica. He hadn't even noticed he'd been doing that, apparently everyone else had. It wasn't that he cared if they knew he was obsessed with her, he was, he just didn't want Angelica to know it yet. He didn't think she was ready. "I guess so, sometimes it just sneaks up on you."

"How long after you hired her did you start making moves?

You two managed to keep it a secret until now, that's rare. I told Gennie that you probably came out with it now just so you could bring her to this event as your date."

"Honestly it's only been recent that we've decided to try this thing out. A couple weeks ago it just happened. When we realized it wasn't going to be a fling, we knew that we didn't want to have to sneak around."

"And she's already living with you?"

"It made sense, her building isn't safe for anyone."

"And when she's pregnant what else are you supposed to do, am I right?"

Levi turned in horror to find Foras standing behind him with their mother, Lamia, on his arm.

"Angie's pregnant?" Gennie gasped and everyone around them seemed to take a collective inhale.

"Fuck," Levi snarled. "What the hell are you doing here?" he demanded of his brother and gave Lamia a tight smile. "Besides telling secrets that aren't yours?"

"It was really Mother's idea, and you know I can deny her nothing," Foras said with a sigh that wasn't all dramatics. Levi knew how convincing their mother could be and Foras still depended on her for a lot of financial support so he was in no position to deny her.

"I wanted to see my favorite son and his new bride," Lamia said smoothly, leaving Foras' arm to lean in and kiss Levi's cheek. "I am *very* disappointed that I had to hear this from someone other than you."

Angelica had walked over just in time to hear that declaration and Levi was tempted to grab her and whisk her away from whatever might be said next. She touched his arm and gave him a small smile before turning to address Foras and Lamia. "We aren't getting married," Angie said with a laugh and rubbed her belly, "but yes, I am pregnant. We hadn't planned to announce that tonight, thanks."

Lamia's mouth tightened at Angelica's show of spine, then it curled up in approval and Levi wasn't sure if he was glad or terrified that his mother thought Angelica might be a worthy match for him.

Levi reached out and grabbed Angelica's hand, wanting to show a united front. Her fingers clamped around his in a lethal grip, her nails biting into his flesh. Maybe she wasn't taking it as well as it seemed.

"This is her?" Lamia asked.

"Mother, this is Angelica Walsh, Angelica, this is my mother, Lamia Blackwood."

Lamia reached out a hand for Angelica to shake and Levi's instincts were to pull her away. He didn't think his mother meant her harm, in fact, his real worry was that his mother would decide that he wasn't worthy of Angelica. There was a special word for demon males who reached out of their league to trap women, and it was the worst kind of insult.

"I'm so glad to finally meet you," Angelica said sweetly and grasped her hand briefly. "And it's so nice of you to be here to support your son. Having this business running so well for ten years now is a big deal."

"Ten years is it?" Lamia asked in a bored tone. "I suppose that's worth celebrating. I'm more interested in the last year and what got you and my son so entwined." Her eyes flared at the words and Levi swallowed. He didn't know what Foras had told their mother about the situation. If she knew the truth, she wasn't here to congratulate, she was here to save face for the family.

"Mother, may I have a dance?" Levi asked and stepped away from Angelica, grabbing Lamia before she could answer and leading her to the dance floor.

"I guess that means you and I should dance as well," he heard Foras say. Levi didn't love the idea of Foras' hands on Angelica, but he couldn't stop it without looking like a dick.

"What a wonderful idea," Lamia said smoothly as Levi pulled her into position on the dance floor.

Levi led his mother expertly around with a firm smile on his face while Foras and Angelica twirled nearby.

"Why are you here?" Levi asked his mother quietly.

"Why did you keep this from me?" Lamia demanded, the smile on her face not faltering. For anyone looking on they would assume that the conversation between mother and son was quite pleasant.

"Because it isn't solid," he admitted with a low growl. He would have told her as soon as Angelica was his, it would be something to celebrate.

"That's what I thought. You tricked that poor girl into having your baby, didn't you? You are a fool and a coward, and I won't have it. My son will not be known for such lowly demon behavior."

He didn't waste any time denying the accusations. "I'm handling it."

"No, you aren't. That girl isn't besotted with you, I can see it in the way she looks at you. There's no love there, only some kindness. I am going to help." She lifted a palm and laid it on his cheek. Her skin heated and he tried not to flinch away from it. "I'll move in with you for a time. You'll need help with the baby so it will make sense. I will talk you up and you will follow my lead. We'll get her to choose you, and no one will have to know that—"

"No," Levi snarled and swung her to the edge of the dance floor, then grabbed her hand and led her out of the ballroom. He took her through the lobby and into an empty bathroom.

"Excuse me?" Lamia gasped.

In the semi-privacy of the bathroom Levi let go of some of his control. His body heated and bulged, his nails sharpened and he felt the tell-tale prickle of his wings. "I said no. I don't want or need your interference, mother. I can manage my own love life."

"Ha! You tricked her, you manipulated her. That is not what a woman looks for in a partner. You'll be lucky if she doesn't leave you and this farce before she even has that baby. What will people say?"

Levi hated that his every fear was being parroted back at him by his mother. He hated that he wanted to say yes to her offer. It would be so easy to let her manipulate things for him and assure that Angie would come to love him in time.

"I don't need your help, she cares for me already, she's just angry."

The way that she'd come to his side in the ballroom when she didn't have to was proof of that. And how she had worried about not looking good enough next to him to come to this party in the first place. Even how she had accepted, with very little complaint, that she was going to be the mother to his half-demon child showed that she had some care for him. It wasn't a lost cause, and he didn't need more manipulation to make her his. He took some deep breaths and brought his body a little more under control. It would only provide further proof to his mother that he couldn't handle things if he lost control and shifted.

He reminded himself that Angelica was too strong to be manipulated by Lamia, and he knew that he didn't deserve her if he couldn't get her on his own. No amount of saving face among the demons would change his mind about that.

Lamia's face softened and he recognized that this was her changing tactics. He braced himself for whatever she was about to say. "Darling, I want you to have everything you've ever dreamed of. I have always wanted the best for my children, you know that." Her sincerity melted his anger, even if it was another manipulation tactic on her part.

"I want that too, Mother. The best thing for me is Angelica and I will get her on my own. I know that I can, even if I started this courtship out the wrong way."

Lamia pursed her lips and the room heated with her anger.

"Fine, but heed this warning. If she doesn't love you before she has that baby, then she never will. Your time is running out."

Lamia stormed from the bathroom and out the front of the hotel. Apparently, she didn't care to wait for Foras. Maybe she'd forgotten he was even there.

Levi hadn't forgotten. "Foras," Levi growled. That spineless idiot had told on him and brought their mother here to mess with everything. Now he was in there dancing with Angelica as if he'd done nothing wrong.

Levi stalked back to the ballroom and swept his gaze around. He couldn't spot Angelica. No bright red hair, no pale skin, no pleasing curves wrapped in black cotton. Panic started to fill him.

"She's in the powder room," Foras said behind him. "She's a good dancer, but I spun her too much maybe. Or it's pregnancy sickness." Foras shrugged as if Angelica being ill was of no importance.

"You're an asshole," Levi seethed, his body heating with anger. He struck out at his brother and made solid contact with Foras' jaw. He wasn't sure if he was hitting him because he'd made Angelica sick, or because he'd brought their mother here. Either way it felt really good and Levi didn't care if everyone who worked for him was watching, which they were.

"Ouch," Foras snarled, his skin tinted red in reaction to the attack. "I'll let that go because I know you've got some unrequited love sickness going on. You know I was only trying to help. Who else could convince someone to overlook what you've done and fall in love with you? Mother is an expert at manipulating feelings after all."

"I don't want to manipulate Angelica's feelings," he whispered, hoping nobody overheard this revealing conversation. "I'm going to find her, and you should be gone when I get back."

Levi wanted to punch more people and things as he stalked to the closest bathrooms. He didn't, because he'd learned at a young age that it was best to keep his emotions in check. Sharon was standing outside the door when he got there.

"Your mother is a real piece of work," Sharon said. "I met her one other time when she came to visit you at the office, scared the shit out of me."

"I know. Is Angelica okay?"

"Yeah, I think she just got dizzy. No one would blame you if you took her home now."

"If that's what she wants." Levi agreed then pushed into the women's bathroom and found Angelica leaning over a sink, rinsing her mouth out. She looked over at him and grimaced.

"Your brother needs dance lessons. I think he thought we were playing ring around the rosie."

"He's an idiot."

"I can't believe our pregnancy was announced like that," she groaned as she dried her mouth. "I knew we couldn't wait too long to tell everyone but I thought we could do something cute like leave an ultrasound picture on the staff fridge or write up a poem and send it out as a memo."

Levi hated that his family had taken that from her. "We still can."

She rolled her eyes at him. "Levi, we've known each other long enough for you to know that I am a 'roll with the punches' kind of girl. My baby isn't human, I am not having an anonymous father for my child, and I am living with my boss who I am fake dating." She shrugged. "So I didn't get to announce the pregnancy my way. I *am* pregnant." Tears filled her eyes and she took a shuddering breath. "Pregnant after so many years of disappointment and waiting. I don't give a fuck if your brother skywrites it across the state. I'm pregnant." Her face lit up with a smile and she let out a little giggle.

Levi realized he had no idea what drove her to the clinic in the first place and he felt like kicking himself for never asking. "What do you mean years of disappointment?"

Angelica looked uncomfortable and he was sure she was going to brush him off. He was glad she didn't. "My ex-husband and I couldn't get pregnant. We tried until we found out that there was a low fertility chance for both of us, so combined it was a no go. I wanted to check out options like fertility treatments or maybe donated eggs or sperm. He didn't think he wanted a baby that bad."

Hurt crossed her features and he wanted to pull her to him and kiss her so much in that moment it was physically painful to stop himself.

"That's when we decided to get a divorce. I just couldn't give up on having a baby, not even for him. I think by that point I was only with him because each month I'd been hoping to be pregnant, we had lost our real connection somewhere along the way."

"I'm not sorry that he didn't want kids, Angelica."

She gave him a shocked look.

"If he had been a better man and willing to do what was best for his wife then I never would have met you," Levi continued. "Nothing in my life has been the same since you walked into it and I don't regret that. I don't regret going to that clinic and I may be delusional, but I think maybe you put the alert on my calendar because you wanted me to know."

"Or maybe the goddess had something to do with it," she pointed out.

"Was the goddess shoving champagne down your throat and getting rid of your inhibitions?"

"Maybe, She is mysterious after all."

He had moved closer to her as they spoke and she hadn't moved away so he took that as a sign. He leaned into her and pressed his lips to hers in a quick, searing kiss.

"Levi," she whispered, her eyes drifting closed and her lips parting slightly for him.

He was tempted to take what she was offering despite the

likelihood of interruption and the less than romantic setting. He wanted to give her more than this though, she deserved better than a bathroom makeout session. "Should we go back to the party where everyone will have questions for us? Or should we go home where we can continue this?" He placed a hand on her hip and squeezed.

She blinked at him as if wrestling with the choice. When she took a deep breath he was already pulling away. "Let's go back to the party, I haven't gotten to eat any of the food yet," she said, her voice thick with emotion.

Disappointment washed through him but he quickly pushed it aside. He was playing the long game with her, it wasn't a race to the bedroom. He gave her hip another quick squeeze and then offered his arm. "Whatever my lady wants."

When they rejoined the party and it became obvious that they weren't running right back out of the place, they were approached by everyone for the next couple of hours with congratulations and advice. Angelica took it all with a smile and her usual cheerful disposition. Thankfully Foras had left, so there wasn't another altercation.

When the night was winding down, Sharon handed Levi the mic and told him that it was his duty to make a speech because this was his big night.

All he wanted to say was how grateful he was that he was looking at Angelica pregnant with his child. Instead, he rambled about how great the year had been and how it was due to all his wonderful employees.

It felt like the type of night that would end in tangled sheets, sweaty bodies, and deep kisses. The look on Angelica's face as he spoke made him think she might feel the same way. He ended the speech abruptly and ushered her out of the room.

As soon as they were seated in the towncar Angelica let out a sigh and put her head back. She stared out her window as they drove. "That was a lot. I'm glad I'll have the weekend to get used to the idea that everyone knows about us. Well, they know what we want them to know," she added with a frown he could see from her reflection. He didn't think she knew he could see her because she lifted a hand and touched her lips. Was she thinking of the kiss in the bathroom?

"What do you want?" he asked her quietly.

"Sleep, I'm so tired and my feet hurt. This baby makes me exhausted," she said without looking at him.

He wanted to push her to answer the question as he'd intended it but she yawned and he stopped himself. His number one duty was keeping her safe and comfortable. If she needed sleep then he'd make sure she got that. Once she was rested he was going to come back to that question.

When they arrived at the penthouse she didn't wait for him to help her out of the car and there was no talking as they rode the elevator up. He'd have sold his soul to know what she was thinking. It seemed to be more than exhaustion that was plaguing her.

"Goodnight, Levi," she said when they walked into the penthouse and then she went into her room and shut the door.

"I want everything," he whispered to himself. If she'd asked, that's what he would have told her.

CHAPTER 19

Angie managed to avoid almost all contact with Levi over the weekend, claiming she wasn't feeling well and hiding out in her room. She was far too confused to face him. She'd leaned into that bathroom kiss, she'd wanted more. Had almost begged him to not take her home or back to the party but to fuck her right there against the sink. She'd been wet and hot, and needy. It was terrifying because she'd felt her heart lurch in a way that she hadn't thought she'd ever feel again. Which meant it was in danger of being broken in a way that she knew would shatter her more than her divorce had.

It wasn't that she hadn't wanted to fall in love again after her divorce, it was more that she hadn't thought it would matter. She'd thought if she had a baby and only ever dated casually the rest of her life she'd be satisfied. Now she knew that was a terrible lie she'd told to protect herself.

The way she ached for Levi went beyond even what could be explained away by the demon fetus thing. She craved his lips and his touch. She wanted to know what he tasted like and what he sounded like when he was unhinged in pleasure. She wanted to know him and she wanted him to know her.

Her vibrator got a very good workout that weekend and she didn't care if he might have heard. If she were being honest, she'd admit that she hoped he did hear. Maybe even daydreamed about him jumping in and finishing the job himself. He never did, and each time the brief pleasure faded she was left aching for something so much more than she could give herself.

Levi didn't leave the penthouse all weekend either and checked on her multiple times. He brought her food which she was happy to eat, and he asked if she needed anything. He seemed disappointed every time she told him no, she was fine just resting by herself. She wanted him to argue a little, she wanted him to demand she leave the room and watch a movie with him, or go for a walk, or even eat at the table. But he just nodded stiffly and said he'd come back for the dirty dishes in a while. And she let him leave because asking him for more seemed selfish and she wasn't sure she could handle finding out that he didn't care if she never left her bedroom.

Sunday night she dreamt of having the baby and holding it in her arms. It was a little boy that looked just like Levi and she was so happy she was crying. Because it was a dream, she was lying in a bed with a canopy on a beach. Levi was standing next to the bed in a suit like he wore to work every day and he was frowning. *I just don't think I want a child that bad.* He said and turned from her to walk down the beach.

The baby in her arms began to cry and Angie tried to call out for Levi to come back but her throat was too tight, nothing would come out. He disappeared and she was alone with the baby who cried and cried, and she knew that it was because it didn't want to be with her, that like his father, and her ex-husband, no one really wanted her long term.

"Angelica wake up," Levi demanded. He hadn't been asleep when he heard her cry out from her bed. For a moment he'd thought she was masturbating, something he'd caught the sound and scent of multiple times over the weekend. He'd nearly come apart stopping himself from going in and demanding to be the one giving her pleasure. When he realized she was moaning in distress this time, he hadn't stopped himself from entering her space.

She was thrashing on the bed and her face was twisted in despair. His heart broke seeing her like that. He crawled onto the bed and kneeled beside her. "Angelica," he demanded again. "Wake up, you're having a dream."

Her eyes flew open and she gasped as she sat up. She looked down at her lap and then at him. He expected her to tell him to get out or demand why he was there, but she threw herself against him instead. She wrapped her arms around his neck and sobbed.

"You're here," she whispered against his neck.

"Of course I'm here, where else would I be?" He ran his hands up and down her back, soothing. Eventually she stopped crying and slumped against him.

"I'm sorry."

"What was your nightmare about?"

She pulled away from him and shook her head. "It was a dream, it doesn't matter."

"Nightmares are not dreams, they are our fears talking to us in our sleep. Angelica," he demanded and waited for her to look at him. When she didn't, he touched her chin and forced her head up. She was beautiful, even with her eyes and nose red, even with her hair a mess from sleep. He wanted to kiss her and make her better, but he knew that it was important to understand what could make her cry out in her sleep like that. "What were you seeing in your head?"

"You left after the baby came. You realized that you didn't actually want to be a dad that much." She pulled out of his grasp and looked down again. "You didn't want to be stuck with me," she whispered.

"That's not going to happen, Angelica. I am not going to change my mind about the child, and I'm not going to change my mind about you." He leaned forward and kissed her. One sweet kiss, no more. He didn't want to take advantage of her emotional state, he only wanted to soothe her. He pushed her gently down and tucked the blankets back up around her.

She didn't argue and when he tried to move out of the bed she grabbed his arm. "Please don't leave me," she begged, her voice cracking with emotion.

Levi felt his heart break at the sound, and he laid down at her side. "I'm not leaving you," he assured her, then rolled her to her side and cuddled into her back. He'd hold her every night if she let him. He couldn't believe she thought he was going to decide he didn't want to be the father of her child.

Maybe he'd been too subtle, maybe he'd been going too slow waiting for her to give him the assurance of her feelings. Maybe she was unsure and needed him to tell her what he wanted for their future.

Levi left her in the early morning. She was sleeping deeply but she made a sound of discontent when he moved and it almost had him going back to her. The only thing that could pull him away was the knowledge that he needed to care for her other needs soon.

He went into the kitchen and started making breakfast. Even though it was Monday they were on a later schedule due to a morning doctor's appointment. There was time for a homemade breakfast and he was going to be sure she had it. All weekend he'd fed her in her room and she hadn't eaten as much as he thought she should. This morning he was going to change that. He was going to change a lot of things.

"Good morning," Angelica said shyly as she entered the kitchen.

Levi had just plated eggs and bacon and fruit. He turned to her with a smile. "Good morning, Angelica. Sit and eat, we have plenty of time before the appointment."

"Oh, yeah I need to shower," she hedged.

"Sit and eat," he demanded and she obeyed. He liked that, a lot. He set her plate down in front of her and then took his own spot across from her. "You need the protein."

She looked like she wanted to say something, but her stomach growled and she started to eat.

"I think I need to explain some demon things to you."

"You mean about the baby? I thought we wouldn't really know a difference until puberty." She touched her stomach.

"About me."

"Is this where you tell me that you have needs and so you can't be expected to not sleep with people even though we are pretending to date?"

"We are *not* pretending," he snarled.

She took a heavy breath. "Then what the hell are we doing?" she snapped back.

"I am courting you. I am going to prove that I am worthy of you and that child."

"Why?" The question was a whisper.

"Because that's what demons do."

Angelica stood up and shook her head. "I'm going to take a shower."

CHAPTER 20

Angelica wasn't sure what to think. Levi had kissed her, twice. He had cared for her all weekend even though she'd ignored him and refused to leave her room. He'd comforted her through a nightmare and held her as she fell asleep. Those were actions that spoke of love, of devotion and caring.

And yet when she asked him why he didn't want to 'fake' date and why he wanted to pursue her, his answer was the opposite. She may not know everything about demons but she knew that they liked to win, they liked to possess things, and they were strategic in their pursuits. It is what made him such an amazing businessman.

She wasn't an acquisition to be strategically achieved however, and neither was her baby.

Was it stupid of her to want it all after telling herself that she didn't need anything more than a baby? She hadn't been touched with such care in over a year as she'd been touched last night and it wasn't even sexual. She'd woken this morning reaching for him, and found an empty bed. Full of hope she'd sought him out in the kitchen, but he wasn't offering her what she really wanted. And she wouldn't settle in a relationship.

With a new determination to keep him at a distance she showered and got ready for the appointment. She dressed in a long skirt and blouse so she could expose her stomach without exposing everything else. She pulled her hair half up and felt confident when she left her room. She found Levi dressed in his usual suit. Today's was a jewel tone blue with a dark blue tie and he looked as amazing as always. His hair was slicked back and his face was freshly shaved. She'd never seen him with more than the slightest scruff and she wondered what he would look like if he didn't shave for a couple of days. Probably devastatingly handsome, so it was a good thing he seemed to shave religiously.

"This doctor you've chosen, they have demon experience?" Levi asked as he held open the penthouse door.

"Yeah, it's the same doctor I would have used anyway, I got lucky that they take demon clients as well."

"Do they know about us?"

"They know I was artificially inseminated with demon sperm."

He didn't seem satisfied with that answer and she didn't feel like elaborating. She wasn't sure what she'd tell the doctor about him. It would be silly to fake being in a relationship in front of the doctor since there were confidentiality things keeping her information safe. She didn't really want to go through the whole explanation though either, especially since she wasn't sure anymore what the truth was.

Levi drove them to the doctor's office. She liked being in his car with his scent surrounding her and relaxed into his soft leather seats. Would her baby smell similar? She supposed that would be something that might come up at puberty when they discovered if they were going to have the demon tendency to flame up or not.

When they parked, Levi jumped out of the car so fast Angie had barely gotten unbuckled. He opened her door before she could even think to try and she accepted his hand out. She didn't move away from his guiding touch at her back until they were inside the building. Then she hurried forward and checked in at the front counter.

"I want my card on file for all charges," Levi said after the receptionist handed Angie a packet of papers to fill out.

The secretary looked confused. "Okay, that's something you'll have to talk to our billing department about."

"I will then," he said and guided Angie to a couple of empty seats in the waiting area.

"What the hell was that?" Angie demanded once they were seated.

"What do you mean?"

"You don't need to pay for my appointments here."

"Yes I do."

"Insurance covers a lot and—"

"I will be paying for anything else," he snapped. People around them started to stare. Angie hated to be the center of attention so she stopped arguing and started on the paperwork. If he wanted to pay, she'd let him pay. He owed her for wasting her bonus on the insemination fee, she just would have liked him to discuss that with her before making assumptions in public.

When she got to the section on father's history she handed him the clipboard. There was no good reason to leave him off.

Levi filled out the required information and delivered it back to the receptionist.

"Angelica Walsh," a nurse called and it was time. She was about to have her first official OB appointment. She looked at Levi who was already standing next to the nurse and she felt something she didn't want to identify. Knowing she was sharing this moment with the father of the baby she carried, sharing this with Levi.

Angie introduced herself to the nurse who showed them back. Her weight, blood pressure, and temperature were all taken. Her temperature was still elevated, but it was reasonable for a half-demon pregnancy the nurse assured her. Then she was asked to pee in a cup.

"Why are you checking her urine?" Levi demanded.

"The doctor will check for protein and glucose as well as infection. It's something we do most appointments as a precaution."

Angie took the proffered cup and gave the nurse an apologetic look. Levi moved as if he were going to follow her to the bathroom and she glared at him. He looked disappointed as he sat back down on a stool.

When Angie returned, he scanned her with his gaze as if he expected her to have been harmed while she was out of sight. She would have asked him what the hell his problem was if the doctor hadn't come in right behind her.

"Ms. Walsh, how are you feeling today?" Dr. Brunswick asked in greeting.

"Good, ready to hear how this is all going," she said and hopped up on the exam table.

"And you brought someone with you today?" Dr. Brunswick held her hand out to Levi.

"Leviathan Blackwood, I'm the father." Levi shook the doctor's hand.

Dr. Brunswick looked from Levi to Angie and down at the paperwork. "Ah, yes I see that here. I'm sorry, I thought you determined it *was* artificial insemination, I didn't realize—"

"Does it matter?" Levi asked.

Dr. Brunswick narrowed her eyes at Levi and Angie wondered if she was about to kick him out. "No, it doesn't. And you're the full demon father so that explains the rapid growth?"

"Yes I am."

"Okay." Dr. Brunswick turned back to Angie and gave her a kind smile. "Your vitals look good. Have you been having the same symptoms?"

"They have gotten better with the anti-nausea medicine. I still have bouts of sickness and my body tends to overheat easily."

"Do you feel like you're getting enough to eat around the sickness?"

"I've been making sure she gets balanced meals with lots of iron and protein rich foods," Levi explained.

"That's great, very helpful. Are you sleeping well, Angelica?"

"Yeah, I haven't had any issues with sleep yet, I know that's coming."

"Yes it is. You'll be up to pee multiple times by the end. Your body is growing more rapidly than it's meant to, so you'll also probably have some stretching and aching so be sure to take it easy when you need to."

Angie nodded. She had felt a tightness in her hips the last few days and she'd been rubbing cocoa butter lotion on her stomach twice a day. She didn't care if she got stretch marks, but she did want to diminish them if she could.

"What kinds of things should she avoid?" Levi asked.

"Other than the obvious, if she feels okay doing it, it should be fine for her. It wouldn't be a good idea to start new exercise routines or push through any sort of pain though."

"I'll make sure she doesn't," Levi assured.

Angie wanted to roll her eyes.

Dr. Brunswick smiled at her as if she thought Levi's attentive behavior was adorable. Angie supposed she was used to dealing with demon patients so his behavior was normal. "Let's take a look at your little one, shall we? Lean back and lift your shirt."

Angie did as instructed and tried not to notice Levi as she lifted her shirt and pushed her skirt down to reveal her stomach. It had never been completely flat, she'd always been a woman with curves and she embraced it. Now it was rounded in a different way and she wondered what he thought of it, and tried not to care. She had no idea what kind of women he was attracted to, she'd always imagined they were all legs and boobs with perfect hair. She dared a glance at him and found his eyes locked onto the exposed skin of her stomach. She'd give anything to know what he was thinking.

His gaze swept up to meet hers. There was a burning there that made her shiver, she felt locked in and she wanted to stay there. She wanted to see what that look could lead to. It felt like the look of a lover, the look you'd see right before you were brought expertly to an orgasm that left you panting and your toes curled. Angie bit her lip and Levi took a sharp inhale.

"Ready to see your baby?" the doctor asked as she squirted gel on Angie's stomach.

Angie broke away from Levi's gaze and turned to the screen the doctor was turning toward them. Soon she was swirling a wand around Angie's stomach and a black and white image appeared on the screen.

"This is your baby," the doctor said, pointing to an alien looking thing.

Angie put a hand to her mouth. Her chest felt tight and tears burned her eyes, she was looking at her baby. She felt Levi's warm hand on her shoulder and knew he was looking at it too. She wondered if he was as mesmerized as her.

"And the heartbeat," Dr. Brunswick said as she flipped a switch. The sound of a quick heartbeat surrounded them.

"It's so fast," Levi whispered and Angie realized he had squatted down so his face was right next to hers.

She reached up and put a hand over his and squeezed. This certainly wasn't what she'd imagined over the last year, and yet she couldn't have been happier. Sharing this with Levi felt perfect.

"It's supposed to be fast," the doctor assured him.

Levi stayed like that while the doctor measured and took different angled images of the alien blob before declaring everything to be growing right on track, *for a half-demon baby.*

When she printed out photos, Levi took them with an eagerness that surprised Angie, staring at them with awe.

"When will we know if it's a boy or a girl?" Angie asked.

"It's a girl," Levi said.

"Excuse me, how do you know that?"

"All half-demons are girls."

Angie looked at the doctor who nodded confirmation. How had she not known that, why hadn't he mentioned it? She grabbed Levi's hand, feeling a little panicked. "What else don't I know?"

"Whatever you don't know, I do, and we're doing this together, remember. I'm not going anywhere, Angelica."

His words, echoes of what he'd said to her last night when she'd been so upset, filled her heart to bursting and she had to blink rapidly to keep the tears away. "Thank you," she said and she meant it. "I'll do some more research, I should have done it already. Things have just been so … fast."

Levi seemed disappointed by her remark. He quickly covered it with a blank look.

"I assure you, that there's nothing you need to prepare yourself for other than a shorter pregnancy. Everything else is very normal until the child is older."

"Then she might start bursting into flames," Angie joked.

"It's not as dramatic as all that," Levi assured her. "At least not at the beginning. There are signs that it's starting and we will teach her techniques to calm herself down. Besides, she might not shift at all."

We, that one word wrapped around Angie and tightened. Was there going to be a 'we' in twelve years? And then her thoughts halted on his other words. "Shift into what?" she demanded.

"I'll leave you two, let me know if you have any questions before the next appointment. Angie, you're doing great," Dr. Brunswick said as she left the room.

"Into demon form," Levi said as if it were obvious.

"You'll have to excuse me if I don't know what the fuck that is, Levi. Demons don't exactly advertise their differences."

He had the decency to look contrite. "It's not that big of a deal. Along with the heightened temperature that can cause a bit of a meltdown under extreme stress, full demons have a larger and darker form that helps us to blend with shadows, and wings."

"Wings!" Angie shook her head as she imagined a tiny baby with wings and how she could possibly get a diaper on it if it could fly around the nursery.

"Angelica, you're panicking," Levi said and put a hand on her chin, forcing her to meet his eyes.

"Yeah, I am having a demon baby and I have no idea what a demon can even do."

"I will show you."

"Okay," she agreed quickly and sat up straighter, ready to know what her child might be capable of.

Levi chuckled, she was certain she'd never heard that before and it caught her off guard. "Not here, not now, but I promise I'll show you at home tonight so you can stop worrying."

"Easy for you to say," she grumbled but hopped off the table and grabbed her purse.

Levi put a hand to her back and guided her out of the building.

CHAPTER 21

Levi was flying high the rest of the day. He'd pocketed some of the photos that the doctor had printed out and taped them to his desk drawer so that every time he looked down he saw what he'd created with Angelica. Every time Angelica walked into his office for something, he stared at her stomach and knew what was there. All he wanted to do was wrap his arms around her and never let go.

By the end of the day he was anxious to get her upstairs. The idea of showing her his other form thrilled him more than he would have expected. It also worried him, because if she didn't like what she saw, he knew she'd never forget it.

"Ready?" he asked at the end of the day. She was still seated behind her desk typing something.

"Yeah, just sending this last message. Do you know why Rachel Tilsdale won't reply to me?"

Rachel Tilsdale was the owner of the waterfront property that he'd been set to develop until he'd had a rather violent meeting with her investor friends.

"I thought I told you, that deal fell through."

Angelica's fingers froze on her keyboard and she looked up at him with a frown. "Why?"

"It just did, that happens in business sometimes."

She narrowed her eyes at him. "What did you do?"

"How do you know I did anything?"

Angelica just looked at him.

"It was when you were refusing to come back to work," he grumbled.

Angelica shook her head and stood up. "You need me more than I need you," she said with a sigh.

Levi didn't even try to argue.

When they got upstairs he tried to distract her with talk of dinner but she refused to do anything before he showed her what he promised.

"Are you certain you need to see this?"

"I'm having a demon baby that might *do* this, Levi, hell yes I'm sure."

He couldn't argue with that so he sat her on the couch and started to strip.

"Woah, is this a naked thing?" Her eyes were wide and she was clutching a pillow.

"Not entirely, I'll keep my boxers on."

Was that disappointment he saw flash across her features. "Okay, get on with it," she prompted.

Levi didn't linger over the undressing, making quick and efficient work of taking off his suit down to his boxers. She'd seen most of this before but her eyes roamed over him like it was the first time, and she liked what she saw. Levi felt like preening under her scrutinizing gaze. He wanted her to like what she saw, wanted her approval. The way she licked her lower lip and closed her eyes briefly before she met his gaze told him everything.

His cock threatened to engorge and he had to pull up his best cock blocking thoughts to keep from really embarrassing himself. It still grew some, and noticeably, judging by the widening of her eyes when they slipped down again briefly.

"I want you to know what to expect," he said to distract them both. "My skin color will change and my muscles will bulge. I'll get a little taller even and my nails get sharp. Wings sprout out of my back."

She nodded and hugged the pillow tighter.

Levi took a deep breath then let his body do what came naturally. Moments later she gasped as his wings spread out behind him.

Angie didn't know what to think, hadn't known what to expect. She had pictured the most horrifying of things, but this … this was beautiful. He looked like a sculpture, all smooth muscles and sharp lines. He hadn't been kidding about his size, he had grown a lot both in height and bulk. She had to keep her eyes far from his crotch where his boxers were doing an amazing job of holding it together while his body fought against every thread. She wasn't sure if his cock had just grown in tandem with his body or if he was fully erect, either way he was massive. Frighteningly massive.

Her thighs clenched and she forced her gaze up to his face. Other than the color change, he was now a deep burgundy, there wasn't much change there. Maybe a slight widening of his jaw. "Are your teeth different?" she asked then covered her own mouth, hoping she hadn't asked a rude question.

He chuckled and grinned wide. "Nope, I am not a sharp toothed monster now. Not about to devour virgins."

Well that's great, because I'm definitely not one of those. She thought and then chastised herself for letting her mind fall back into the gutter.

"Can I see the wings?"

He turned slowly, allowing her a view of him from all sides. He even flapped the wings a couple times, moving air around the room. When he was once again facing her she thought she saw worry in his eyes.

"I can't believe more people don't talk about this, it's amazing."

His shoulders relaxed and his wings folded in. "Not many know. We didn't want to freak out the humans with too much too soon, and then I think most demons decided it was nice to have something that was ours away from the fanatics."

Angie could understand that. There were always groups of humans who were obsessed with another species to the point that it could sometimes become dangerous for the supernaturals. Seeing Levi like this, she had a feeling that he'd develop his own cult following instantly if anyone knew.

"Thank you for trusting me," she said.

"I don't want to hide anything from you, Angelica. I want you to know all of me."

Angie wanted that too. She stood up and walked to him slowly, hoping this was okay. He didn't move a muscle as she approached so she reached out and ran a hand down his arm. His skin felt hot to the touch, even more than normal for him and his muscles underneath were rock hard. "May I?" she asked, indicating his wing.

Levi didn't answer but spread them out once more. They looked like leather but when her fingers stroked them she found they were soft like velvet. They vibrated slightly at her touch and she pulled her hand away with a gasp.

"Sorry I—" she began.

"No, it's just that, no one has ever touched my wings before, I didn't expect them to be so sensitive."

"Oh," she said and felt her face heat noticing that his cock was now without a doubt fully erect between them. She wanted to be brave, she wanted to reach out and stroke him, she wanted to invite him to do things to her that she'd been fantasizing about.

Then her stomach growled and he was suddenly shifting back to his human form and grabbing for his clothing. "Dinner time," he said, his voice gruff.

"Yeah, I guess so."

Before he moved away he grasped her chin and bent to press his lips to hers. It wasn't the passionate kiss he'd given her in the bathroom but it wasn't the quick comforting kiss he'd given her last night either. This was something else, something more and it reached a part of her heart that she thought had been locked away.

"Thank you for letting me show you all of me," he whispered against her lips then walked away leaving her a burning mess of emotions and desire.

Angie was exhausted by the time dinner was done so she didn't argue with Levi when he encouraged her to head to bed and let him take care of cleanup. She felt like they really needed to have a discussion about what had been happening between them. She knew that he was attracted to her, but she also knew that he was most concerned about the baby and that she was taking care of herself during pregnancy. His libido had been cut off like a faucet when her stomach had growled. He wanted to take care *of* her, that didn't mean he really cared *for* her or wanted her. She also had to remember that the baby made her want to be around him which could be confusing her own hormones. Sure she'd daydreamed about her sexy boss before she'd gotten pregnant, and even masturbated to mental images of his scowling face a few times. Did that mean she had a chance to develop real feelings for him now that they were living together?

She was terrified that the answer was yes and she was doing

exactly that while he was not. She needed to keep some space between them.

"I'll do what's best for you, don't worry little angel," she whispered to her belly.

After she was tucked into bed she texted her sister pictures of the ultrasound and told her it was a girl.

Oh my goodness! A girl! I am so excited and will be sending you lists of names every day for the next ... how long is this pregnancy?

I will appreciate the name help, I have been thinking about it all day and have only come up with names I definitely hate like Mildred and Fanny. The doctor today gave me a due date of June 14th.

Mildred! Ugh, yeah you need help, don't worry I got you sis and I will buy tickets to be there, you are not allowed to have that baby without me.

Angie realized that was another discussion she needed to have with Levi. Did he want to be in the room? She scoffed because that was a stupid thought. With the way he was acting, of course he would. Did he want his mother in there? Would he be offended if she said she needed her sister in there? She stopped herself from thinking about Grayson and how he'd told her once that he kind of hoped he'd miss the birth because he thought it would be super gross.

"I can't believe I ever thought he was ready to be a dad," she grumbled.

I will expect you here for sure.

Angie didn't make any promises on whether or not Henley would be in the room when Angie gave birth.

CHAPTER 22

Sleep didn't come easy that night even though she was tired. She was afraid she'd have another dream about her ex, and she was lonely. "Are you doing this to me?" she asked her little angel. "You think we should be near your dad?"

Angie refused to make an embarrassing trek to Levi's room so she tossed and turned and hardly slept. When her alarm went off in the morning she was feeling like a zombie. She dressed in leggings and a loose dress, not caring that it was unprofessional, it fit and it was cozy. She threw her hair in a bun and tried to cover the circles under her eyes with makeup.

It didn't work well apparently because when she met Levi in the kitchen he gasped.

"What's wrong?"

She glared at him and wished she had something to throw his way. "I didn't fucking sleep."

"Why?" he demanded. "If you had more bad dreams you were quiet about it."

"You have to sleep to have bad dreams," she mumbled and pushed him out of the way so she could pour a cup of coffee. Today was not the day to forgo the caffeine.

"You don't have to come to work if you don't feel up to it."

"Sure, and have everyone say I am getting special treatment because I'm fucking the boss, no thanks," she snarled.

Levi looked taken aback by her words and she almost felt bad. It wasn't his fault that she hadn't slept. Except it kind of was. He had done this to her and his stupid demon DNA was making her want to be next to him. She glared at him harder and he took a step back. Good, she shouldn't be the only one suffering through this. The worst part, she didn't think it was all about the baby anymore, she actually wanted to spend time with him, she wanted to see where those kisses could go. She wanted her demon boss.

"Is there anything I can do for you, Angelica?" he asked carefully.

Angie sighed and drank the hot coffee. "No, I'm sorry." She gave him a half smile.

"You don't need to apologize, your feelings are valid and you're tired because your body is doing amazing things."

"Yes it is," she agreed and walked to the front door. Levi quickly followed.

When she walked by Sharon's desk the woman made a commiserating sound. "Pregnancy is rough sometimes, you not sleeping, hun?"

"Not last night," she admitted.

"Well maybe you should try some different positions. You know, tuck a pillow between your knees or something. Body aches can ruin sleep and boy does a baby make the body ache."

Angie smiled at Sharon, the woman was a saint. "Thank you, I'll give that a try."

"Oh, and Levi if you are too far from her she won't sleep well, you know the baby makes her need the father around."

Angie cringed at Sharon's words, why the hell did she have to point that out? She took back her mental saint comment, the woman was definitely a troublesome demon.

"Is that true? You aren't sleeping because you want to be near me?" Levi asked, hurrying to catch her as she speed-walked to her desk.

"You're the demon, not me," Angie mumbled and dropped her bag on her desk. "I need the bathroom," she said and hurried away so he couldn't ask her about it anymore.

When she got back to her desk Levi was behind his own. She made his coffee and checked the calendar for the day then went in to give it to him the same as she'd done every work day.

"You can work in here today," he stated as if it weren't an unusual request.

"No, I need to be at my desk where all of my things are."

"You need to be near me," he hissed.

"The baby needs to be near you."

"And you are pretty attached to it right now so what's the difference?"

"The difference is that I don't want to be more attached to you, Levi. I don't want to feel these things for you because I don't think they are going to disappear when the baby comes out. What if yours stop when it does? I don't think I can handle that."

He looked stunned at her admission and so she walked out. It was more than she had wanted to admit to him, but he wasn't getting it any other way. The man could really be dense sometimes.

The rest of the day went on like usual and although Angie was more tired than normal, she didn't take any of Levi's hints that she could go upstairs and nap, or leave early. She could tell others were watching, that they saw how tired she was and were going to judge if she took special privileges. So she wouldn't. And besides, as long as she was busy at work she didn't have to think about how embarrassing what she'd spouted out to Levi was. Maybe he hadn't caught that she was starting to fall for him, because she hadn't been so sure until that moment. She needed a little space so she messaged Patrick that they were going out for tea and talk after work.

He immediately replied with a thumbs up emoji and a meme of two girls jumping up and down in excitement.

Levi was disappointed when Angelica informed him that she was going out with Patrick after work for a quick *tea and talk* as she called it. He was glad she had someone to talk to, even if his instincts screamed at him to keep her away from everyone else until their relationship was solid. He sent a picture of the ultrasound printouts to his mother and as expected she called him immediately.

"Does this mean she's accepted you?" Lamia asked as soon as Levi answered.

"No, it means your grandchild is growing on track, I thought you'd like to know."

"Of course I want to know, I also want to know that Angelica isn't going to make a fool of you, Leviathan."

"She's not demon, she doesn't understand things the same way I do. For her, moving into my space doesn't mean she's accepted my courtship, or me." He hated how true that was but he still had hope, especially now, after the things she'd said to him in his office.

"She may be human, but she knows that having a baby together will force a relationship of some kind."

"It wasn't her choice and that relationship could be platonic co-parenting."

"It was her choice to go through with it," she pointed out. "She wants the baby, now make her want you."

Levi wanted to yell at his mother, he managed to take a deep breath instead. "I am making progress. I know that she has feelings for me, attraction at least. She is understandably cautious."

"Then you are not proving to her that you are a good mate, Leviathan. What have you done to prove yourself?"

"I cook for her and she's living here for free. I anticipate any need I can."

"That's a start. What about making her feel like it's a permanent place? If she doesn't feel secure in her space she can't feel secure about you."

He hated to admit his mother might be right. He said a curt goodbye and hung up, then walked around the penthouse. It had never been a space he particularly loved. He did like it better now after the few changes he'd made. He didn't know if it was what she wanted though. He didn't want to ask Angelica what she'd like to change because he knew that she'd say it was fine and it didn't matter, because she didn't think she'd be staying. He needed to anticipate what she would like and give it to her, that's what a good mate would do.

Levi planned as he made dinner. When Angelica arrived he'd just finished setting the table with pork chops and a spinach salad.

"This smells great," Angelica said as she took her usual seat.

"And it will provide lots of needed vitamins for the growing baby."

Angelica rubbed her stomach and smiled softly. It was the look of a mother and knowing he was the father responsible filled him with pride. He wanted to talk to her about what he was feeling, and planning, and wanting. The only thing that stopped him was that she looked tired still, more tired than last night or this morning. She couldn't do another night without good rest, and he knew exactly how to fix that.

"I'd like to watch a movie with you tonight after dinner," Levi said as they ate.

Angie looked up from her meal. "A movie?"

"Yeah, I thought we could switch up our usual routine." And if she fell asleep next to him, all the better. "I'll let you pick the movie," he said when she still didn't respond.

"Really?"

"Of course."

"Oh, okay, yeah I can do that." She tried to hide a yawn as she spoke and he ignored it. If he sent her to bed like most nights, then she would just not sleep again.

"Wonderful. I'll clean up while you pick."

Levi was almost giddy as he cleaned up the kitchen and met her on the couch. He'd never had a date over here for a movie. He'd had them over for sex and drinks. Never a meal and definitely never to hang out. So sitting on the couch with Angie was a new experience for him and he was very glad that he'd already replaced it. Angelica had gotten a blanket off of her bed to cuddle up in. It was one that he recognized as coming from her apartment and Dalton had delivered in the boxes he brought up. She'd also arranged a few pillows around her that must have come from her apartment. It gave him an idea of what he could do next, how he could make her feel more comfortable in this space.

She picked a movie quickly and it sucked her in. Soon she was droopy-eyed and Levi pulled her legs up on his lap. Her body slid down onto the pillows she'd brought out.

"What are you doing?" she asked, coming wide awake.

"You look uncomfortable." It wasn't a lie, and this had been his plan. She needed sleep and she needed him with her when she got it. He would make sure that happened.

And he would love every second of it. His fingers itched to caress her, but he didn't dare. He merely held them where they had landed after he moved her. It was contact, he'd take it and he'd relish it.

Levi sat through the rest of the movie even though she fell asleep halfway through. She didn't wake up as he moved her to his bed, she was finally getting the sleep she needed and that filled him with satisfaction.

CHAPTER 23

Angie woke up slowly, confused. It smelled like Levi's house and somewhere in the distance she thought she could hear her alarm. It was muffled though, as if it were in another room. She moved and her body slid against sheets that were softer than she remembered and her arm slid against a fabric quilt she didn't recognize.

Her foot twitched and hit against someone. She shot up and looked around. This wasn't her bedroom, or the guest bedroom in Levi's house.

"Angelica, good morning."

Angie looked over at Levi's sleepy morning face and she gasped. Had she slept with him? She clutched the blanket to her chest and tried to remember what happened. They had been watching a movie on the couch. He'd had her lay down and then, nothing.

"What happened?" she demanded.

Levi sat up and the blanket dropped to pool around his waist revealing his tattooed chest. It was a mouthwatering sight and didn't ease Angie's worry at all.

"Angelica," he said soothingly. "You're completely dressed, same as you were on the couch, what do you think happened?"

She looked down at herself. Despite having the blanket clutched to herself like she was nude, she could tell that she was in fact wearing the leggings and T-shirt she'd changed into after work. "Oh."

"Yeah, I am a little disappointed that you think you would be able to sleep through sex with me."

"More like I could have been too tired to know what I was doing," she mumbled.

"And that you would think I would do something that you weren't enthusiastically into."

Angie cringed because he was right, she didn't think he would ever take advantage of her or anyone else like that. "Sorry, I am not quite awake. I think I heard my alarm."

"It has been going off in the other room for a while. I was just debating if I should wake you or if I should let you sleep in."

"Never let me sleep in unless it's the weekend."

"Noted."

"Um, so why am I in your bed?"

"Because the baby won't let you sleep well if you aren't next to me."

That wasn't the answer she'd wanted, but it was the truth so she nodded. "Oh, thanks. You don't have to do that though, we'll work it out." She patted her stomach for emphasis.

"No, Angelica, you won't. This is what's best for you and the baby right now so this is the new situation. We sleep together so that you can rest and stay healthy. It would be stupid to do anything else."

Well, when he put it like that could she really argue? Did she want to? "Okay," she agreed.

"Great, you shower and I'll make breakfast." Levi got out of the bed and she was relieved to see he was in a pair of basketball shorts.

Of course when he turned to the side she wasn't sure it really was better than him being nude because his cock was bulging out of that soft fabric like it was about to get a ride. Seeing him like this and not being distracted by his demon form made it impossible to look away.

"Angelica?" Levi asked and when she jetted her eyes up to his she saw amusement there. "I asked if you want coffee this morning or herbal tea."

"Tea," she squeaked out.

Levi chuckled dark and low, then walked to his own attached bathroom. As soon as the door shut she jumped out of his bed and ran to her own room, then took a cold shower.

Angie couldn't even look at Levi the rest of the day. She avoided him as much as possible and when she had to interact with him she looked over his shoulder like the most interesting thing in the world was behind him. She was thankful when he left the office after lunch for some business meetings. And too relieved to realize there were no meetings on the calendar until she was heading upstairs alone at the end of the day.

When she walked into the penthouse she noticed changes right away. There was a lamp from her apartment set up where the glass bowl she'd broken once sat. She turned to the living room and found her favorite couch blankets stacked neatly in a basket. There were throw pillows she recognized as having been hers as well as a photograph of a field of lavender hung on a wall where he'd previously had a black and white print of a cityscape. It was a picture she'd taken when she was a teen and was really proud of. There was even a rug on the floor in a paisley purple print that hadn't been hers but she loved and would have bought in a heartbeat if she'd had a living room large enough for it.

It reminded her of everything she'd dreamed of one day having for her and her child. It was large but not too big for a small family, classy while still being comfortable, and with so much light for her plants. How had he known? It was as if he'd picked the images out of her brain and made them real in his home. Tears burned the backs of her eyes.

"I hope you don't mind. I brought up a few of your things from storage."

"Why?" she asked without turning around. She didn't want him to see how glossy her eyes had become or how hard she was gritting her teeth to keep back the emotions.

"Because it was time for me to nest and I want you to be comfortable here in more than just your bedroom."

"Nest? So is this your style?" she asked doubtfully.

"A demon usually nests with his mate in mind when he is going to have a child and this is what I see when I think of a home with you and our daughter."

She didn't know what to say to that. What did it mean?

He grabbed her hand and pulled her to the kitchen. "Dinner is ready."

Angie sat at the table and he served her on plates she recognized as ones she'd picked up at a thrift store when she'd first moved into her apartment. They were cheap and cute, and nothing like the white and silver set he usually used that likely cost a fortune.

"Do you like eggplant parmesan?" he asked when he sat.

Angie nodded and began to eat. As usual it was delicious, he was an amazing cook.

"Do you want to watch another movie tonight?"

"Sure, you can pick tonight though."

"Perfect," Levi said.

After dinner they both changed into lounge clothes and settled on the couch. It was warm and cozy with her blankets and pillows on it, she felt at home. It was getting harder and harder to remember that this wasn't home. That his vision for their future wasn't clear to her, and so she wasn't sure it was what she could accept. Did he expect her to live here with their daughter forever? Would she be a permanent guest in his home until they sent their daughter off to college? Did his kisses mean as much to him as they did to her?

"Angie?" Levi prompted and she realized he was holding the remote out to her. "I just can't decide, will you pick?"

"Oh, sure." She grabbed the remote and picked the first movie that looked interesting. It ended up being a great movie, if she'd been alone with her vibrator … Who knew there was so much sex involved with a bank heist. By the third erotic scene she was ready to die of embarrassment and Levi was sitting stiff beside her, refusing to look away from the screen. She didn't want to admit there was anything wrong with her choice, or that she found it disturbing in the most erotic way to watch these sex scenes with him.

By the time the movie ended Angie was so wound up she thought a slight breeze would bring her to orgasm. There was no way she could sleep next to him tonight, she needed her vibrator.

"That was a fun choice," Levi said, clearing his throat.

"Um, I think I'll head to bed on my own tonight, I don't think we need to share."

"Okay, sleep well." He said, surprising her with his lack of argument.

Angie got up and hurried to her bedroom before she could do any of the naughty things she'd envisioned while sitting with Levi on the couch. As she closed the door of her bedroom she thought she heard him groan.

She went straight to her bedside table and pulled out her favorite dildo with the vibrating thumb. Levi knocked on her door so she threw it on the bed and hurried to see what he wanted.

"You forgot your phone out there," he said, holding it out to her.

"Thanks." She held out her hand for her phone but he was looking at something behind her. She didn't have to turn to know what he was looking at and she felt her face heat with mortification. She wanted to melt into the floor, she wanted to push him out the door and slam it between them. Maybe not ever look him in the eye again. She wanted .... She wanted to grab him by the shirt and drag him into her room and use him to relieve this ache between her thighs instead of what he was looking at now.

She tried to grab her phone but instead of letting go of it, he moved forward when she pulled. Suddenly their bodies were touching and his eyes were boring into hers. There was desire burning there, more intense than she'd seen even when he kissed her in the bathroom at the company party. She could feel heat radiating off of his body and unless it was a trick of the light, his skin seemed to darken.

"Levi, I—"

"Angelica, if you are in need, I can be of much better assistance than that purple appendage."

"I don't think that's a good idea," Angie insisted even though she didn't really feel that way. She wanted what he was offering, she wanted it badly.

"I think it's a very good idea," Levi said and leaned down. He pressed his lips to her cheek, then her earlobe and whispered there. "I want to strip you down and do so many dirty things to you. Angelica, I want you so much I'm burning up inside with desire. My cock has been hard for you since you walked into my office over a year ago.

It was everything she wanted to hear even if she didn't believe him. His hands ran up and down her sides and he groaned deeply in appreciation when they reached around and grasped her ass. He pulled her to him and she felt how hard he was for her, or maybe the movie had gotten to him too. She didn't care about how it happened, she just wanted what it could lead to right then.

"Oh fuck, Levi," she gasped when he rocked into her. "Yes, please," she said when he did it again.

"Can I have you, Angelica? Can I strip you down and worship you? Can I show you what pleasure only I can give you?"

"Yes," she said eagerly, even nodding her head in case she had unknowingly lost the power of speech. Her heart was racing and her body was tingling with need. She might regret this in the morning, but right now she didn't care. She wanted to experience him.

That one word set him free from whatever had been holding him back. He scooped her into his arms and carried her as if she weighed nothing. She wrapped her arms around his neck and pressed kisses below his ears, he tasted like he smelled and it was intoxicating.

"Do you taste this good everywhere?" she asked.

He groaned and hurried his steps. He wasn't taking her to her bed though, he walked out of the room with her and down the hall then into his bedroom. "I told you that you sleep here now," he growled as he shut the door behind them then laid her down on his black duvet.

Finally, his lips found hers.

The first touch was lightning and hot as fire. It burned slightly and she didn't care, she felt like he was marking her, making her his and she wanted it. Her hands wrapped around to grasp in his hair and hold him close as she opened her mouth for him. His tongue was a lick of flame in her mouth, branding her from the inside. She groaned and arched off the bed as he devoured her mouth. His hand slid down, easily slipping into her pajama pants and panties.

"You're soaked for me, Angelica, aren't you?"

"Yes," she groaned as he slipped one finger between her lips and deep inside of her.

"So fucking hot. I bet you taste just as good here as you do here," he said, licking at her mouth.

"I—I don't know," she admitted.

He chuckled and slid down her body, pulling her pants and

panties down, quickly discarding them. He ran his hands back up her thighs and pushed her legs wide. On his knees between hers he stared down at her pussy with a wicked grin. Then he leaned down and gave her one long slow lick from ass to clit. He sat up just enough to meet her gaze and she swore his eyes were burning red now and his skin had definitely changed tone. It wasn't quite the maroon it had been when he showed her his other form, but it was on its way there and she suddenly worried that he might completely change during sex. She didn't know how she felt about that.

Good! Very good, her mind screamed.

"Even better than I imagined," he confirmed, then dipped his head back down and began a slow assault of her sex that was unlike anything she'd ever experienced before.

It distracted her thoughts because she didn't know what to do. It wasn't the first time a man had gone down on her, however she had never felt like the guy was enjoying it this much and no man had ever been this good at it. She squirmed on the bed, her hands gripped the headboard above her and she bit her lip to keep at least some of the sounds from escaping. When his tongue dipped low and circled her asshole she flew up and grasped his hair. "Levi stop, I can't take any more."

He let her lift his head and kissed her stomach. Then he pushed up her shirt and kissed it again. "You can take everything I want to give you, Angelica, trust me."

She wasn't so sure. She thought he might just devour her or make her combust and she'd die in a sparkly, pleasure-filled burst.

He pulled her shirt off and kissed her mouth again. She tasted herself there and shivered.

"I told you, you taste good."

Angie wanted to be embarrassed by that, but she couldn't be anything other than turned on. His hands ran over her like he was worshiping the most precious of statues and his kisses were so sweet and possessing, she couldn't imagine him ever wanting to stop. He was everything she'd ever dreamed of finding in a lover.

"Why are you still dressed?" she groaned against his mouth as her hands plucked at his shirt.

"I like how impatient you are for me."

"It's not like I haven't thought about what this would be like," she admitted.

"I hope I can live up to your daydreams."

Levi hopped off the bed and stripped quickly. Angie leaned up on one elbow and took in her demon boss completely nude for the first time. He was bulging more than usual and his skin was even darker.

"Are you going to sprout wings?" she eyed his hands. "Or claws?"

He lifted his hands and inspected his fingers. "No, I won't shift completely during sex, it's more intentional than that, or brought on by extreme anger or violence." He met her gaze and his eyes blazed. "The passion I feel for you doesn't come from a place of violence."

Angie shivered at the intensity of his words. Her gaze ravaged his fully naked body now that her concern was alleviated. She couldn't move past his cock, fully exposed and fully engorged. It was bigger than any she'd ever seen in real life and it scared her a little. She swallowed and darted her gaze up to his. "Um, condom?" she asked because she didn't want to tell him to stop, she did trust him, she knew he wouldn't hurt her.

Levi reached into a drawer and pulled out a condom. Before he could open it, Angie popped up on her knees and took it. She moved fast so she couldn't second guess her skills and dropped her mouth down, taking his cock in deep.

He sucked in a quick breath and his hands slipped into her hair.

"Angelica," he groaned.

She slid him as deep as she could down her throat then pulled back up and ran her tongue around his hot tip. He tasted good here too and she groaned as she took him deep again. She reached with one hand between her thighs, the ache too much to ignore and began to circle her clit.

"No," Levi growled and lifted her off of his cock. He pushed her gently back on the bed and crawled between her legs. "That is my job, naughty girl."

She shivered at his words and wondered if she had some kink she didn't know about.

His hand replaced hers and he stroked her until she was panting and clutching at him. It took an embarrassingly short amount of time. She was wound up by him and probably the pregnancy hormones too, so she was on the edge fast. She could tell it was going to be a big one. "Please, oh god, please Levi, I can't."

"I know, baby." He took the condom she'd dropped on the bed and quickly opened the package and rolled it on, all while kissing her so deep her head spun. "Are you ready for me?"

"Yes."

"Look at me," he demanded.

She met his eyes as he slid into her. "Good girl," he rumbled and her pleasure ratcheted up another notch.

His body was so hot, so unlike anything she'd ever experienced before. It stretched and burned and felt so good she wanted to cry. She kept her gaze locked with his as he demanded and saw his eyes flare red and black as he filled her.

"Levi," she gasped as he sunk all the way in.

"Angelica, I don't think I ever want to pull out," he said with a smirk, then he began to slowly pull back and move forward with a sharp push. Again and again he moved like that, teasing her body and building pleasure without giving enough until she was ready to scream. She grasped at his shoulders and pressed her nails in, then bit her lip and lifted her hips. He didn't change his movements though, just kept up with the slow assault on her nerves until she thought she might die for real.

"Tell me, baby, tell me what you want."

"Harder Levi, I need it harder."

"Anything for you."

Levi wrapped his arms around her and buried his face in her neck as his body began to piston rapidly in and out of her. It was a bruising rhythm and exactly what she needed. She felt her orgasm coming and she didn't hold back.

"I'm so close," she cried out.

Levi slipped a hand between them and barely touched her clit before she exploded. The fiery pleasure rocked through her. She felt him take hold of her hips and his movements became erratic as he raced to his own orgasm.

"Angelica," he cried out and shuddered before collapsing and rolling them to the side. He held her close as their breathing slowed and the realization of what they'd just done settled.

She'd just fucked her boss.

CHAPTER 24

Levi was in heaven, absolute bliss, holding Angelica in his arms and knowing he'd given her pleasure. It was the single best moment of his life and satisfied the demon instincts to claim and mark her as his. He ran his hands up and down her back and kissed her shoulder. He felt her shudder and his cock twitched inside of her.

"Don't move," he instructed, then rolled away from her and disposed of the condom. He brought back a warm cloth from the bathroom. "Let me," he said and nodded toward her thighs.

She hesitated, he could see the indecision on her face and he was about to tell her she was being ridiculous when she parted her thighs. She was absolutely stunning here. He thought he could spend a lifetime worshiping between her thighs and never get bored. His mouth craved another taste of her.

"L—Levi?" she asked and her legs started to close.

He moved quickly so she couldn't, snapped out of his reverie he swiped her clean with a gentle touch. He couldn't help himself though, he leaned down and kissed her red curls.

"Levi," she squealed and pushed his head away.

"Too delicious to leave alone," he said with a grin. He tossed the rag toward his hamper and crawled into bed with her. Then pulled the blanket up and reached out, pulling her close. He kissed her and nipped at her bottom lip. "I love having you in my bed."

She gave him a worried look. He rolled her over and tucked her into his chest wanting to soothe whatever her mind was telling her. He kissed her head and held her until she was breathing deep and even and he knew she'd fallen asleep.

Once he was sure she was deeply out, he laid a hand on her slightly rounding belly. It was warmer than the rest of her body, already their daughter was showing signs of her demon heritage and it filled him with pride. He whispered all the things he wanted with them both. He laid out his entire soul to her and prayed to the chaos goddess who had gifted him this miracle that Angelica would see him as a worthy man to have those things with. His only purpose, according to his mother and nearly every other demon alive, was to find a woman who would allow him to impregnate her and care for her. He hadn't thought he had that drive before he met Angelica. He had actually thought there was something wrong with him because any time he'd seen a demon woman on the lookout for a mate he'd been turned off. Then Angelica had stepped into his office and he'd felt all his demon instincts come to life. For a year he'd ignored them and tamped them down, but no more. Now that he'd had her, now that she'd allowed him into her body, he could let all those instincts out. He could open his heart to this amazing woman, he just hoped she wouldn't break it.

He fell asleep with her wrapped in his arms and slept well for the second night in a row. When he woke up and she was still there he felt like he had won something. She woke slowly and blinked at him in confusion at first then her cheeks reddened.

"Good morning, Angelica."

"Hey."

"Alarms are about to go off, but I'm the boss so we could go in late."

"You know I don't want people talking about us and now," she paused and covered her face with her hands. "Oh god, now they're right. I slept with the boss."

"You are really worried about what they think?"

"I'm worried about so many things," she said with a sigh and got out of the bed. Levi just watched her go, unsure what to say to that. How could she be worried about anything after they'd shared such pleasure? Did she not feel the same insatiable draw that he did? Perhaps she needed more assurance, he needed to prove that he was committed to this courtship. He needed to make a claim to her in demon society so she knew he was serious. Lucky for him, his mother had sent an invitation last week he'd planned to pass on but maybe he wouldn't.

Later they sat across from each other at his desk. She was absolutely beautiful. Her hair was wild and she kept pushing it out of her face so he knew it was frustrating her. She'd been rushed this morning, thrown off of her usual routine, and had not taken the time to pin it up. It gave her a look of such whimsy that he hoped she didn't decide to tame it. He was tempted to crawl over to her and pleasure her right here in his office. He was sure she'd object, so he didn't.

"I'd like to take you to a little party tonight."

"A party? It's kind of late notice."

"My mother stayed in town and she's having a little gathering tonight. A dinner and drinks sort of thing."

"I guess if you need to go it makes sense that I'd go with you, if we want everyone to believe we're dating."

Levi barely held back a snarl. How could she think it was still fake after last night? "Angelica I—" His words were cut off by a knock on his door.

"Levi motioned in Mrs. Williamson and then the meeting that they had been waiting for commenced. Angelica took notes as he and Mrs. Williamson discussed the remodel of her high-rise apartment building.

The rest of the day was busy and he didn't have a chance to speak with Angelica again until they were back in the penthouse.

"So about the party," Levi began but then the door buzzed.

"Who could that be?" Angelica asked.

"I ordered something," Levi said as he hurried to the wall and hit the button. "Hello?"

"I'm here with dress selections for Ms. Walsh."

"Dress selections?" Angie asked.

"For the party. I just thought you might like something new. I meant to bring it up earlier. I can tell her she isn't needed if you had something in mind to wear."

Angelica looked nervous. "No, it's fine, let her up. I guess if I have the right dress I won't feel so awkward about going to your mom's party."

It wasn't exactly the answer he'd wanted, but it was a start. He let the woman up with the dresses because if Angelica knew what this party was really about, he had a feeling she'd never agree to go.

Angie had never had clothes delivered before unless she'd ordered them online. She was nervous about what Levi might have requested, and sizes too. She was a curvy woman and pregnancy was already starting to make those curves more lush. It wasn't going to be easy to find something elegant like she assumed was required for his demon mother's party.

"Are you sure it's a good idea to go to this party?" Angelica asked.

"I am sure that she'll be less likely to stop by here if we go to her party."

Angie wasn't going to argue with that reasoning.

Levi opened the door and let in a short woman with spiky

blue and black hair and an eyebrow piercing. She was dressed in jeans and a T-shirt that somehow looked edgy and designer at the same time. She was pulling a rack of dresses that sparkled in every color of the rainbow.

"I'm Helen, and you must be the luscious and lucky lady that is getting a new dress."

"I guess so," Angie said and shook the woman's hand.

"Wonderful. I'll leave you two to it and get myself ready." Levi kissed Angie's cheek and walked to his room, leaving Angie alone with the dresses and the edgy designer.

"I'm happy to help you, Angelica. Mr. Blackwood was emphatic that you have every choice available for the occasion."

"Angie," she corrected with a half-smile.

"These are my designs so if you don't like something, be nice," she said with a laugh. "Just kidding, they are mine and I won't be offended if they aren't your style, everyone is different."

"Wait, Helen Gillespie? Owner of High Designs?" It was the sort of shop she didn't even dare look into because it was so expensive.

"The one and only," Helen declared. "Now, let's get started, we have a lot to try and not a ton of time." She looked Angie up and down and nodded. "Mr. Blackwood described you perfectly. I think you'll find something here you'll love and feel amazing in."

That surprised Angie and she was still doubtful when she started looking through the rack of dresses. After a few minutes of browsing Helen sighed heavily.

"What are you looking for? What do you like?"

"In fancy dresses I can't afford?" Angie laughed.

"Mr. Blackwood assured me price wasn't an issue," Helen pointed out. "Let's start with colors and fabrics."

"Purple is my favorite, all shades. Nothing with sequins, sorry I don't want to feel like a disco ball."

Helen looked thoughtful for a moment then pulled out a

couple of dresses. "Try these and tell me what you do and don't like about each, it will help me narrow down what you want."

"This feels like an episode of *Say Yes to the Dress.*"

"Sorry, I don't do bridal," Helen said, the sarcasm lost on her.

Angie went into her room with the dresses. Helen tried to follow but when Angie gave her a startled look she stepped back into the hall. "Let me know if you need help zipping or anything."

Angie tried on five dresses before she found one that she felt truly beautiful in.

"He's going to drool when he sees you in that," Helen assured her.

"That's not—I mean, I didn't pick it for him."

"Sure, well if you ever need anything else give me a call, I've got his credit card on file now," Helen said with a wink.

Angie got ready and tried not to think about how right Helen had been. She did want to see Levi drool over her in this dress. He'd been so professional and regular all through the day and she'd started to doubt whether or not he felt the things he'd seemed to last night. He was taking care of her the same as always, yes, but last night she'd thought their relationship was becoming something more. She'd felt truly beautiful and cherished in his bed. Then today it was back to just caring if she ate enough protein and if she was feeling ill. She seriously thought if he asked her one more time if she was feeling nauseous she might just puke on his shoes.

She wanted more with him. There was no denying that now, and it scared her because what if he didn't?

She washed and straightened her hair, slicking it back into a smooth ponytail and applied her makeup a little more smoky than usual. When she put on the dress, she knew she'd chosen right. It was a floor length deep purple chiffon with a slit up to her waist. Underneath the dress she wore a gold bodysuit bustier that peeked above the low sweeping neckline of the dress. A braided gold belt went around her waist and she'd put on a pair of gold sandals that laced up her calves. The overall look made her feel like a goddess, and the power of a goddess is exactly what she thought she needed to face Levi's mother again.

Levi knocked on her door as she stared at her jewelry box. "May I come in?"

"Yeah, I'm almost ready," she said and turned as he opened the door. He was in a tux with a purple bowtie that perfectly matched her dress, Helen must have told him.

"Oh my god," Levi gasped.

Angie's heart started to pound and her palms felt sweaty. "Is it okay? I don't know if I have the right jewelry for it."

His eyes locked onto hers and she saw a flash of desire there so strong she felt it rock her core.

"Angelica, you are exquisite." He held out a large jewelry box. "Helen said gold would be what you needed."

She hesitated. She had already accepted too much from him. She hadn't seen a price on the dress though she could guess, and it was ridiculous. "I'm sure I have something."

"Please, Angelica." He opened the box and she gasped.

It was simple and elegant and exactly what she had been wishing she had. A thick gold choker and drop earrings. It would enhance her dress without distracting from it. She nodded and took the earrings, fastening them on. When she reached for the necklace he pulled back.

"Let me," he said and she turned so he could hook the choker around her neck.

His fingers were hot and sent a shiver down her spine when they brushed her skin. She met his gaze in the mirror and knew he was feeling the same thing as her. The temptation to tell him they should stay home and just fuck all night was almost irresistible. He seemed to read her mind because he leaned close and kissed her neck then just below her ear.

"This dress is too perfect to waste on just me. Just know that I'll be looking forward to taking it off more than staring at you in it all evening." He laid a hot, open-mouth kiss to her shoulder then stepped back so she could turn.

"Levi—" she didn't know what to say. "You look great too," she decided on because anything else felt too heavy.

He ran a hand over her stomach which was hidden in this dress, one reason she'd picked it. "I hope to make you both proud," he said, his voice gruff with emotion. Then he offered her his arm and they were on their way.

CHAPTER 25

"Is this a rental or does your mother keep a house here?" Angie asked when they pulled up to a mansion in the hills. It was lit up and there was music flowing out with people everywhere and Angie's nerves returned.

"This is one of a few properties she owns. She likes to bounce around, this isn't somewhere she usually spends a lot of time. Obviously she wants to be close while waiting for the baby," Levi explained.

"Great," Angie said and touched her stomach.

"Don't worry, I won't leave your side.

"And I won't let her think we aren't a couple," she assured him.

He looked like he wanted to say something to that but the driver stopped in front of the house and it was time for the party. Levi got out and she didn't even try to open her own door, she just slid across the seat and let him help her out.

He put a hand on her back and led her toward the house.

"Are they all going to be demons in there?"

"Mostly yes. Don't worry, demons are not the judgmental type. Unless you're a witch," he added with a grunt.

Angie's nerves were high and she leaned into Levi for comfort as they swept into the house. It was full of people laughing, drinking, and dancing. There was a live band somewhere she guessed by the sound being piped throughout the house. It was a fast and dark music that surprised her. She would have expected something to elicit waltzing, then again, these were demons so maybe she shouldn't have been surprised by the music choice.

Angie was glad to see that everyone was as dressed up as her and she wanted to thank Levi again for the dress because if she'd gone with her black cotton one again, she'd want the ground to open up and swallow her whole right now. At least she looked like she belonged here in this dress, even if she didn't feel like she did.

"Angelica," Lamia gushed and hurried forward to embrace her. "I am so glad you are here."

"Thank you for inviting me," she said, looking at Levi, uncertain what to do with her attention.

Lamia held her tight and whispered in her ear. "You honor my son, Angelica."

She didn't know what to say to that so she just smiled, and when Lamia released the embrace, she grasped Levi's arm.

"Yes, she does," Levi agreed, apparently having heard the words.

"Can I make an announcement?" Lamia asked.

"Oh, I think everyone knows I'm pregnant, don't they?" Angie said with a nervous laugh.

"No," Lamia hissed and leaned in close again. "No, no, you keep that to yourself dear," she said with a tight smile. "Unless you're ready to announce that you have chosen him, we don't need it getting out what he did." She glared his way, then slipped an arm around Angie's back and pulled her away. "Let me do some introductions. These are very important people to the family, all very close. They don't swim in the circles of Levi's employees, so I assure you they don't know what he did, let's keep it that way. As far as they know, Levi is beginning a courtship and you've accepted."

"That's all true," Levi assured his mother from behind them.

Angie looked back and saw that Levi was trailing them with a murderous look on his face despite his calm words. *It's okay,* she mouthed to him. If she had to pretend whatever nonsense here to make Lamia happy and keep her off of Levi's back, then she would.

He just shook his head.

"Raum, I want you to meet Angelica Walsh, Leviathan is courting her well. Angelica this is my brother, Raum."

Raum was a large man with a bulging face and a receding hairline. His suit looked expensive and his watch was so shiny with diamonds it nearly blinded Angie.

"Finally, Leviathan has found someone to put his attention into. I hope he's making a good showing, Angelica. Just because you are a human doesn't mean you don't deserve the full treatment from him. Make him work for it," Raum said with a wink. "A demon is only worth as much as he shows during the courtship."

"Uncle Raum," Levi said coldly and shook the man's hand, diverting his attention.

Angie was stupefied and it didn't get much better from there. She was swept around the room and introduced in much the same manner to many people who all made very similar comments about what she should be getting from Levi during this apparent courtship.

The whole thing left Angie reeling and by the time Lamia was distracted enough to leave them alone, Angie was begging Levi to take her for air and get her something to eat.

Levi hurried to meet her needs. He took her out to the back garden which happened to be where the rock band was set up and playing. There were plenty of people out there, but they were a younger crowd all dancing and having a great time so they didn't even give Levi and Angie a second look.

Levi urged her past the crowd and they found a bench in the garden to sit on. He handed her a plate of food he'd managed to bring out with them and she started eating immediately.

"That was a lot," she grumbled around a bite of cheese and prosciutto. "I am not sure if I feel like a prize horse being appraised or the buyer of one who is being convinced to give the old nag a chance," she said with a wink.

Levi's face flushed. "Most demons are married by my age and already have a child or two so yeah, you're with a horse past its prime in their eyes. I guess I didn't think to warn you."

She shook her head. "I don't get it. Why were they saying all that stuff about you proving something to me? About courting me? That feels much more serious than dating."

"Aren't we more serious than dating?" He asked, looking meaningfully at her stomach.

The baby, that was what all this was about and as much as it hurt her, she needed to keep that in mind, she needed to keep her heart protected.

She had an awful feeling it was already too late for that.

"Yeah, the baby means we won't just decide we don't work and never see each other again," Angie said with a forced laugh.

Levi wasn't sure how to respond to Angie. Every time he thought she understood that he wanted her, that he was *courting* her, she acted as if they were still playing some kind of game. Had she not heard his mother introduce her as his courted female all night? It tightened his insides with anxiety. He needed her to know that this was real for him, just not here, not now when there were so many prying eyes and ears. This was a discussion they apparently really needed to have, alone.

They made an early exit. When they got home, despite how much he wanted to peel that beautiful dress from her body and make love to her again, and how much he knew they needed to have a serious conversation, he could tell how exhausted she was. He convinced her to lay down in his bed with him and cuddled her to sleep instead. He managed to keep his cock down until morning when he woke up craving her taste and didn't want to resist it. If they were a little late to work it was okay, Sharon knew that they had been at his mother's party and there were no expectations of him this morning.

He felt her start to stir beside him, so he kissed his way down her body, feeling her come more awake with each press of his lips. He spent extra time at her belly whispering words of love and encouragement to the baby inside while he waited for her to be fully aware.

"Levi, what are you doing?" she asked sleepily.

Levi didn't answer, just slipped lower and showed her. He nipped at her lips and clit through her thin panties until she was wet and squirming. Her hands found his head and held him close. If she'd pushed, even a little, he'd have stopped, but she pulled him closer. She wanted this as much as him. Her legs parted and he pushed her panties to the side, diving in with his tongue and lapping up the taste of her. It was something he knew he'd never get enough of.

"You taste like the sweetest fruit," he murmured against her and she giggled.

"You taste like smoke," she said.

He sat up and frowned at her. "Is that bad? I'm not sure I can do anything about that. I'll try. Perhaps if I—"

"No!" She sat up and kissed him deep, letting her tongue prove her point. When she pulled back she looked deep into his eyes, her caramel gaze still soft from sleep. "I love your taste."

She pulled him down on top of her. They made love slowly until they were both spent and panting.

"Are you sure we have to go to work today?" Levi asked, his face pressed against the top of her head.

"I know that you have a meeting this afternoon with Mr. Miller."

"He's an idiot."

"Yep."

Levi sighed, then promised her coffee and breakfast if she joined him in his shower. She didn't need much convincing and although he'd planned to wash and pleasure her, she dropped to her knees under the hot spray and took him in her mouth as if it were her favorite thing to do and how could he argue with that?

God she was amazing. He knew he couldn't lose her and he was terrified he would.

They arrived at work a few hours late and no one commented, at least not that he noticed, and Angelica gave no signs of distress.

That peace continued for another week and he was in heaven. They made love every night and he took care of everything she needed at home. She took care of him at work, something he had thought might be hard for him once they entered into a relationship. He found it was just another way to care for her because she enjoyed her job. She liked being good at what she did, so in a way, letting her care for him in the office was just another way to care for her. He also avoided having the conversation that he knew they needed to have.

He didn't want to rock the boat. She may not know that he wanted this forever, but she had to feel what he was feeling, right? She had to know that he was in it for so much more than the next couple of months and then a part-time parenting deal. Each day that passed and she didn't start nesting in his penthouse he knew that she didn't understand. She kept things neat and clean, she put everything away and made sure that, like sweeping her desk into its drawer each afternoon, she left no trace of herself behind for him to see. His demon instincts screamed at him that she wasn't his, but they offered him no solution. He became desperate and consulted some online dating advice forums. All they seemed to care about were getting a woman to sleep with you and not become attached, what the hell was wrong with human men?

Angelica seemed content enough and talked about what kind of birth she wanted, while making his part in it seem optional. She talked about names and didn't ask him for options, only his opinions on what she liked.

He saw the problems, he saw the holes, and he tried to fill them with orgasms and dinners and desserts while he contemplated his next moves. He even arranged a quick trip to the beach for an overnight. Anything to make her see that being with him was something she'd want forever. And still she made no mention of the future beyond the birth, made him no promises, and asked him for none. What would she do if he offered her everything?

Two weeks later during a late Sunday breakfast there was an unexpected buzz at the penthouse door.

"I didn't order anything," Angie said with a shrug.

Levi went to the intercom and pressed the button. "Yes?"

"Is this the asshole demon who tricked my sister into having his baby?" the voice demanded.

"Henley?" Angelica asked, hurrying across the room.

"Yeah, let me up," Henley demanded.

Angelica nodded at Levi. He hesitated only a moment before buzzing Henley into the elevator that would allow her up.

"I better go put something on," Angelica said and hurried to her room. She'd been in one of his shirts and nothing else. He'd been five minutes away from crawling under the table and having dessert to distract them both from the pressing questions of the future. Now he didn't know what was going to happen and he was kicking himself for not talking to her when he had the chance.

CHAPTER 26

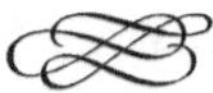

Angie wasn't sure how she felt about her sister being here. Why hadn't Henley told her that she was coming? And why did it have to be now, when she and Levi were in such a good place? Even if it was mostly a physical way. They hadn't had the deep conversations that they needed to. So she still didn't know where they were headed. He'd said things here and there, always spur of the moment, passion-filled sorts of things, not real declarations. He'd also not pressed her on what she wanted for her future or with him possibly. She had to assume he wasn't ready for that yet. He definitely wanted her around, which was the whole reason they were in this situation, wasn't it? He hadn't wanted her to leave her job, or to have to push her away because she smelled like some other guy, so he'd manufactured this situation they were in.

It wasn't the sort of scenario that led to a permanent relationship.

She shook the thoughts away and focused on getting dressed. Her body was still thrumming from this morning's sex and she had been looking forward to more, so her mind was definitely not thinking straight. She'd never been touched with such reverence, never been pleasured so thoroughly before. It's not like she'd never had good sex, she had. This was different and she couldn't even really explain why. Must be a demon thing, she decided.

She took a fast shower and pulled on some jeans that didn't quite button anymore and a loose shirt that hid the fact. Her hair went up into a bun because she didn't have time to wash or style it. When she rushed out of her room she found Henley standing in the kitchen with a cup of coffee in hand that Levi must have just brewed. Levi was nowhere in sight so she imagined he'd gone to get dressed as well since he'd been in lounge clothes at breakfast.

"Henley," Angie squealed and ran into her sister's arms. "Oh my god, it's so good to see you."

Henley pulled back and grabbed Angie's face, searching it, then pushed back further and took in her whole body. "You are showing," she finally said.

"Yeah, a little."

"I guess that's normal for a half-demon?"

"I guess it is."

Henley pulled her in tight again then whispered in her ear. "Are you okay? We can leave right now. I'm not afraid of a demon baby daddy."

Angie laughed and pulled away. "I'm good, Henley, I promise. And I am super glad you're here, I've really missed you." Tears sprang to Angie's eyes and she couldn't even blame the pregnancy hormones. Over a year had passed since she'd seen her sister last and that was the longest they'd ever been apart.

Henley wiped Angie's face and her own eyes glistened. "Hey baby sis, don't worry, I'm here now and I can be for as long as you need."

Angie led her to the living room where they sat and caught up on Henley's life. Angie asked question after question to deflect from talking about her own situation. That only lasted until Levi reappeared in a pair of gray slacks and black button-up shirt, obviously freshly showered. His hair was slicked back looser than usual with a few locks falling forward as if he'd been rushed to get back out here.

"You met, I guess," Angie said awkwardly.

"We did," Levi said as he sat across from them.

"He claims that you're happy here and free to leave at any time," Henley said.

"That's true," Levi said and looked at Angie who could only nod. She may be free to leave but she didn't have anywhere to go. She was happy because the sex had been great. That didn't mean she was feeling like this was a permanent situation though, which when she really thought about it, was upsetting.

"I'm not leaving until I'm convinced, or she agrees to come back home with me," Henley declared.

"Of course, you're welcome to stay as long as you'd like. I don't have an extra bedroom but I can set you up at a nice hotel nearby," Levi explained and Angie was thankful he didn't say anything about her room being available since she'd been sleeping in his for the past few weeks.

"Oh no, I'm good to share with Angie, we're sisters."

Angie only nodded, because she couldn't exactly tell her sister to go somewhere else. "It wouldn't be the first time we had to share a room," Angie said tightly.

Levi narrowed his eyes at her.

"I guess this means you'll have to go to your mother's party alone tonight," Angie pointed out.

"Your mother? You are dragging Angie into your family events like some kind of trophy you knocked up?" Henley accused.

Angie watched Levi's face harden before he masked it with a calm she recognized. It was accompanied by the smell of sweet smoke.

"Why don't I make you some tea?" Angie said quickly, hoping to defuse the situation.

Levi's eyes darted to her and he shook his head. She never should have told him about her trick. "Angelica is not my trophy, she is the mother of my child and she is my—"

"Your what?" Henley demanded.

Angie wanted to tell her it was none of her business, except she was wondering the same thing.

"She's whatever she wants to be," he finally answered. It felt flat and it wasn't what Angie was hoping to hear.

"And if she wants to be not here with you?"

"Like I said, she isn't my prisoner, she's free to leave."

"Great, let's go, Angie."

"Go?"

"Lunch or something, we need some air where we can talk."

Angie looked from Levi to Henley, unsure of what she should want right now. Levi sat stoic and Henley stood, holding out a hand to her. Angie wanted Levi to argue, wanted him to say something that would show that he thought of her as more than just the mother of his child and a convenient fuck.

He just sat there looking like this was a business meeting that was not quite going his way but he wasn't that invested in it anyway so he didn't care.

"Okay, let me grab my purse." Angie tried not to show how hurt she was as she stood and walked to her room. She grabbed her purse and met Henley at the door. "Not sure how long we'll be," she called out as she hurried her sister out of the penthouse and into the elevator while the smell of smoke grew thick.

Once in the elevator Henley turned to her and huffed. "You have feelings for him," she accused.

Angie broke down in tears and her sister wrapped her arms around her. She sobbed all the way down to the ground floor then wiped her face and laughed. "I shouldn't, I know. He's so fucking sweet to me and I know he cares. I know that he wants to be a father too, I just don't know that he wants me and this baby forever. He hasn't talked about it and I worry ..." she trailed off and Henley nodded.

"You're worried that he's going to wake up one day and decide he doesn't really want to be a dad all that much."

"Yeah," she whispered. "Or that he just doesn't really want me."

"He's courting you though, right? It seems obvious to me. Don't you know about demon culture?"

"How do you?"

"I asked around," Henley said as if Angie were an idiot. It reminded Angie of when they were kids and Henley had to explain literally anything to her younger sister. She loved knowing more and making Angie feel like she knew nothing.

Angie didn't admit that she'd only researched half demon pregnancies, assuming there was no need to dive into the intricacies of demon relationships. Maybe she should have. "It doesn't matter what the demon culture says," she argued. "He hasn't asked me to marry him, he hasn't said we are going to be together forever doing this baby thing. I don't even know if I'd believe him if he did," she admitted.

"Are you hungry or do you want to just walk?" Henley asked soothingly.

Angie laid her head on Henley's shoulder and grabbed her arm. "Let's go to the beach, there's a great little coffee shop and we can sit in the sand."

Henley nodded and they walked to Angie's car which had been parked in the garage since Dalton had dropped it off. Angie hadn't had the need to go anywhere alone that she couldn't walk to since she'd arrived on Levi's doorstep. She wasn't sure if that meant she was comfortable in his home, or just that he was constantly around to take her wherever she needed.

As they drove Angie pointed out all the places she liked. They found some beachside parking then walked a short distance to

Mooncalled Coffee, a little shop she loved. It had the best coffee and the nicest owners.

After they had their drinks they walked to the beach and watched surfers on the water.

"What do you want with Levi?" Henley asked.

"I don't know, he's sexy and great in bed."

"You didn't tell me you're sleeping with him!"

Angie bit her lip, that had slipped out. She had never kept things from her sister, it was shocking she hadn't spilled that part already. "Yeah, for a couple weeks now."

"I guess I'm not surprised," Henley laughed. "He's fucking hot, you'd have to be a saint to resist that demon."

Angie laughed then sighed. "He's also the father of my child, and my boss. He's a rich eligible bachelor too, I see the way other women look at him. I just don't think he's going to be happy with me, not forever."

"And you're preparing yourself for him to leave you in the lurch by keeping yourself from pressing him for those answers?"

Angie didn't like that her sister could see right through what she was doing with Levi. "I am protecting myself, Henley, I have to."

"So why not come back to Montana with me? Just start over the way you wanted, you and the baby."

Angie's stomach turned at the idea, the baby rejecting the thought of leaving her father. Angie's heart ached, rejecting the idea of leaving Levi. "Because I think I'm in love with him," she admitted.

"That's what I thought," Henley sighed and put an arm around Angie.

She leaned into her sister's comforting touch. "What the hell am I going to do?"

"You are going to be brave, and you are going to ask him to tell you exactly what he expects to happen, and if you can't live with what he tells you, then you are going to come home with me. I will hire a moving company to do everything and you will never have to set eyes on that demon again."

Angie sniffled. "You're a really great sister, even if you are a little pushy."

"I know."

They spent the afternoon together then Angie dropped Henley off at her hotel. Which Angie should have realized her sister had already booked because she didn't show up at the penthouse with luggage.

"Angie," Henley said and grasped Angie's belly. "I can't believe you are finally realizing your dream. I know how long you've wanted this and I have wanted it for you just as long. I couldn't be happier I just—"

"I *know*," Angie insisted. "I love you too and I will call you if I need anything and you'll be here when the baby is born."

"I'm not leaving until tomorrow afternoon, I expect to see you before I leave and I expect you to tell me how that conversation went."

Angie nodded. "I'll be here to take you to the airport. I am okay, I'm a big girl."

"I knew that bastard Grayson never wanted to have kids," she blurted.

Angie stepped back.

"He told Charles that he didn't want kids at the bachelor party. I thought he must have changed his mind when you started trying but there were other comments. Things about how relieved he was when you started having issues getting pregnant. I'm so sorry I didn't tell you," Henley said, tears in her eyes.

Angie couldn't believe what she was hearing. How could her sister have kept this from her? "Why didn't you tell me?"

"You were happy, Angie you were so happy, and I never thought he'd do something like that."

"Me neither and I was married to the man. I don't think I would have believed you even if you'd told me, I was too excited to have a baby." Angie touched her stomach. "And that's what I'm doing. I don't know if I'm doing it with the right guy and I don't know if he'll stick around. But no matter what, I will have this, and that's what I've wanted for so fucking long."

"Oh Angie." Henley wrapped her in a hug. "Have fun at the party tonight and I'll see you tomorrow."

Levi was panicked. Henley had taken one look at him and apparently decided he was unworthy of Angelica. She could right now be leading Angelica onto an airplane that would take her away from him. He'd thought they were making progress, he'd thought there was plenty of time. What if he was wrong, what if she didn't think he could take care of her and their daughter?

He'd wanted to take her to his mother's party tonight confident that she was his. Up until Henley walked in the door he had thought that's exactly what was going to happen.

He had no idea if Angelica would even come back. Henley obviously didn't think much of him and he couldn't blame her. He knew he'd gone about things wrong but not for the wrong reasons. His feelings for Angie were deep and she'd forced him to face it with the whole artificial insemination thing.

He was planning an airport confrontation when the penthouse door opened and Angie walked in, alone.

He rushed to her and pulled her into his arms.

"Um, hi?" Angie said.

"Where's Henley?"

"She's at her hotel. I told her I would give her a ride to the airport tomorrow."

He pulled back and looked her over. She looked upset but she gave him a smile. "What happened?"

She shrugged and pulled out of his grasp. Levi followed her to the living room. "She brought up some really good points."

"What kind of points?" Levi asked darkly.

"That I'm afraid of asking you about the future because I'm afraid you don't want what I want. And I'm afraid that even if you do now, you'll change your mind later. Maybe I don't get demons, or maybe you're just like my ex, but you haven't told me that you want this permanently and that leaves me thinking."

Anger filled Levi at Angie's reminder that she'd been married to an asshole who hadn't known what kind of jewel he'd had. "I want you, that is not changing."

"I'm so scared that it's going to happen again." Angie looked at him with tears in her eyes and Levi's heart broke.

How could she think he was going to change his mind? "Haven't I shown you? What more can I do to prove that I will be a good choice for you?" he nearly roared the question and she looked stunned.

"A good choice for me?"

"Yes, I have been waiting for you to choose me, Angelica. I have been trying to prove that I can take care of you."

She shook her head and held up a hand. "Is this a demon thing?"

He stiffened. "It is."

"Well, I guess it's not the 1800's anymore so a girl can choose a guy as much as a guy can choose a girl. That doesn't mean I want to."

"What are you saying, Angie?"

"I'm saying that if you expect me to tell you that I want to spend the rest of my life with you and raise our daughter together happily ever after then you are sorely mistaken. I am not getting down on one knee and proposing to you, Levi. I am the woman and I am human and I expect you to do that sort of thing." Her voice cracked and her eyes glistened.

He smiled at the little fit she'd just thrown. He had half expected her to stamp her foot at the end of it. Then her words sunk in and he gasped. "You want a happily ever after with me?" Levi asked, daring to hope.

"Do you love me?" she asked.

"Yes! Yes, Angelica, I love you. I think I fell in love with you the first time you walked into my office. I know I trapped you into having my baby, I know I hijacked your life and created this scenario where you are living with me and it wasn't really fair. I also know that I love you and I would do anything to make you happy. I want a forever with you, I want you to choose me, Angelica. I chose you already, I guess maybe I forgot to send you that memo."

"Oh Levi," she sobbed and ran into his arms. "I don't know when it happened but I fell in love with you too. I didn't care as much as I should have that you hijacked my insemination and I was fine with the excuse to move into your home. I liked pretending to be your girlfriend and more. I love you, Leviathan Blackwood and I want to make a real life with you and this little girl."

"You're choosing me?" he whispered, needing to hear the words.

"I chose you a long time ago, I just didn't put it in my calendar so it didn't feel official."

"Your calendar?"

She laughed and pulled out her phone then typed something. She held it up and showed him her calendar where there was an important event for the day highlighted in gray.

Start living the life you deserve with the man who loves you.

CHAPTER 27

Angie was showing, there was no way around that and she didn't want to hide it anyway. Helen had once again provided her with an amazing selection of dresses a few days before and Angie had picked one she felt good in. It was black with sequins around the hem. It hugged her body to her hips then flared out to the floor. It had two slits up the front and showed lots of leg when she walked. She couldn't wait to see Levi's face when she showed him. She turned in front of the mirror and admired the way it emphasized her stomach. There had been no doubt in her mind that she'd be revealing her baby bump tonight. Now, after her and Levi's confessions of love and a rather quick and hard round of lovemaking, she was also sure about revealing their relationship.

"Wow," Levi said, coming up behind her and wrapping his hands around her front to settle on her belly. "You look amazing. I think I'd rather stay home and celebrate some more."

"And have your mother show up tomorrow ready to raise hell? No thanks, we will go and we will show off. She won't have anything to complain about."

Levi huffed. "She always has something to complain about, but this will definitely shorten the list."

Angie turned in his arms and was surprised to see him in a plum tux with a black bowtie. "Oh wow."

"I thought you'd be in purple too, we'd have matched."

"I thought you'd be in black," she laughed.

He leaned down and kissed her nose. "You have no idea how happy you made me today."

"I think I have an idea," she said and pushed her hips forward, feeling his hardening length.

Levi growled, "Be careful baby, I don't need any convincing to push up that dress and fuck you against the mirror."

"Later," she said, a little breathless. "I know how important tonight is." Levi had confessed to her that tonight was supposed to be their announcement party, though up until a few hours ago he hadn't been sure they'd have so much to announce. He'd also slipped a ring around her finger that had burned more than a little as it went on and she had a feeling it wouldn't just come off. It was silver with an amethyst at the center surrounded by black diamonds. It was stunning, and thankfully she never wanted to take it off.

"We still did it in the wrong order and some of the older demons are going to scowl about it. Don't let it bother you, they're just old school and think you shouldn't get pregnant outside of marriage."

"Do they also think you shouldn't trick someone into having your baby?" she teased.

Levi laughed and grabbed her chin lightly. "If you want to tell our whole story tonight, I will sit there happily and admit that my worst fear had been someone else filling you with a baby and it drove me so insane that I'd done the only logical thing a demon could do."

"And you think they'll forgive that?"

"Yep, because they will all know that they would have done the same thing in my situation."

They got to Lamia's house on time and Angie was glad that there were about half as many people this time. All eyes locked onto her belly first then slid to her hand, which she kept prominently displayed. She didn't want to cause any trouble for Levi.

"Angelica," Lamia exclaimed when she saw them. She was wearing a red dress that sparkled with gold in the light and hugged her body like a second skin. It was cut low, revealing a lot and Angelica almost blushed seeing her future mother-in-law like this. Her black hair was in loose curls around her shoulders, and her makeup was dramatic and dark. She looked far younger than her age and Angelica wondered if that was a demon thing, or a botox thing.

"Mother," Levi greeted and his grip on Angie's waist tightened.

Lamia ignored Levi and embraced Angie, pushing him away slightly in the process. "He told me that you've chosen him, really truly chosen him," she whispered in Angie's ear.

"I have," Angie agreed and met Levi's gaze over her shoulder. He looked embarrassed and she knew it was because he'd told Lamia that before it had actually happened. She wondered what he would have done if she hadn't confronted him about their relationship.

"Splendid." Lamia ushered Angie to the front of the room where a woman was singing.

The woman stopped when Lamia motioned at her and took the mic.

Angie wasn't sure what was about to happen. She looked at Levi who had been right behind them and he just shrugged as if it were inevitable.

"I am honored tonight, to announce that someone has *finally* chosen my oldest son, Levi. They are not only planning an elaborate wedding—"

Angie stiffened, that was definitely not what she wanted to plan.

"Mother," Levi warned in a low tone.

Lamia ignored him. "They are also expecting! I am going to be a grandmother at last."

Cheers erupted in the room and then there was a mass of congratulations for her and Levi. It was at least fifteen minutes before there was enough of a break in the well-wishes that she was able to beg Levi to find her some food.

Levi settled her at a standing table then went to make her a plate.

"Angelica, I am so glad to see you again," Foras said, joining her at the table.

"Foras, I didn't think you were here, why didn't you come congratulate Levi after the announcement?"

"I don't need to curry favor with my mother by sucking up to her oldest son. That doesn't mean I'm not happy for you two though, he's been a lonely asshole for too long. Ever since he hired you I was waiting for him to make a move. I guess now I know why he never did."

"Why?"

"Because a demon won't pursue a woman he wants as a true mate until he's ready to make that full commitment. There was no scenario where he would have just fucked you out of his system and I think he knew that the moment you walked into his office."

"What are you telling her?" Levi demanded when he arrived with a plate of food for Angie.

"Oh you know, just expressing my joy over the coming nuptials. Am I going to be the best man, because I have already started planning the bachelor party. You like vampire strippers, right?"

"I do not," Levi snarled and Foras laughed.

"Ah, well, it was worth a thought. So what *are* you two planning for the big day?"

Angie met Levi's gaze and smiled. She didn't really care, all she wanted was to be his.

"Something intimate," Levi said, his dark gaze locked with hers.

"Oh thank god, I do not want a big wedding with all these people. Sorry," she cringed a little. "I know they are all, or mostly, related to you, but your mother's idea of small is way too big and I can't imagine what her idea of grand would be."

"Likely insane, good choice. Maybe you two should elope."

"Or maybe we should get married in Montana," Levi suggested.

"Oh, Levi," Angie gushed and reached out to touch his arm. "That is the second best idea I've heard all night."

"What was the first?" Levi asked, leaning close and talking in that low growly way that made her panties wet.

"When you leaned me over the armrest of the couch," she whispered.

Levi's chest rumbled and Angie licked her lips.

"And then what did he do?" Foras asked, taking a slow sip of his wine.

Angie straightened and scowled at her future brother-in-law. She'd forgotten they weren't alone for a second there. Levi's gaze had that effect on her. It drew her in and locked her in place until everything around them faded away.

"I think I need to get my fiancée home," Levi said, stepping away from the table and offering Angie his arm.

"Are you sure? We haven't been here very long."

"We accomplished what my mother wanted, she won't miss us now."

Angie grabbed a few crackers off the plate then Levi's arm and nodded at Foras who tipped his glass to her.

"Welcome to the family, sis."

When Levi was holding Angelica in his arms that night and listening to her sleepy breathing he let a few tears fall. They were tears of joy and of relief because for over a year he'd known that he'd never be satisfied without having everything with the voluptuous woman who had walked into his office. And he'd been terrified to admit that anything less would mean a lifetime of regret and loneliness.

Levi leaned down and gently kissed the top of her head, not wanting to wake her up. She made a noise and snuggled closer to him. She was currently wrapped in his arms with her head against his shoulder and when she moved, it brought her expanding belly up against his side. He wasn't sure if it was wishful thinking or his imagination but he felt movement there under her skin.

"Hello, daughter," Levi whispered and laid a hand on Angelica's taut skin. He felt it again, the smallest brush. A part of him wanted to wake her up and ask if she felt it too and another was happy to have this first moment of bonding with his daughter. "I'll always be here for you both. There's nothing I'd rather spend the rest of my life doing."

CHAPTER 28

They called in to the office the next day so they could take Henley to the airport. Angie had assured Levi that he didn't have to take the day off and that she'd be happy to go in after she dropped her sister at the airport. Levi said they could both use a day before they had to face everyone at work. She thought he was exactly right because when she walked in with this ring, there would be questions, especially from Patrick and Sharon who knew how this whole thing had started. Although, she had a feeling Sharon wouldn't be all that surprised.

They went for lunch before Henley's flight. Angie told her a brief version of what had happened when she got home last night and Henley seemed mildly appeased but still skeptical.

"I am going to be here for the birth," Henley said as they ate pizza.

"If that's what Angelica wants," Levi agreed.

"Levi and I haven't talked about who we want in the room when I deliver."

"Angelica, it's whatever you're comfortable with. As long as I'm there, I don't care who else you want in the room," Levi assured her.

"And your mother?" She had been afraid of having this conversation because she didn't want to tell him that she didn't want Lamia in there.

"Do *you* want my mother in the room?"

"In the hospital, sure. Not in the room if that's okay."

"Angelica," Levi said, grabbing her chin and forcing her to meet his gaze. "it's whatever you want. I need to be with you to welcome our daughter into the world, that's the only demand I will ever make about the birth."

"I want Henley in there with me, she's all I've got—aside from you and her," she looked down at her stomach. "Wow, my family is really expanding fast."

"You deserve this," Henley said quietly and when Angie looked at her she saw tears in her sister's eyes. "Angie, you know that you deserve this family, right?"

Tears stung Angie's eyes and she shrugged. "I guess so."

"I know," Levi said firmly. "You deserve everything you want out of life."

"Thank you Mr. Blackwood," she whispered and kissed his lips.

"Oh my god, you're going to be Angelica Blackwood, that sounds so fancy, like an actress or a model, definitely not a secretary. You aren't going to continue being his secretary are you?"

Angie glanced at Levi. "I guess that's another thing we haven't talked about."

"What the hell *have* you two talked about."

"We love each other," Levi said and there was nothing else that needed to be said right then.

After they sent Henley off to her plane they spent the rest of the day doing some baby shopping and nursery planning. Another thing that they hadn't talked about.

"Did we make a mistake?" Angie asked as they sat on the couch and Levi rubbed her feet.

"I think the maple crib will look nice in the nursery."

"No, I mean we got engaged without talking about so many details of how we want our lives to go. Do you want me to still be your secretary?"

Levi moved his hands up her legs and gripped her thighs through her leggings. "Do you want to still be my secretary, or do you want to do something else? Or nothing? You could be a stay at home mom. I can take care of you and her and everything else."

"I like working, and you know that I would never subject another poor woman to the horrors that being your secretary entails."

"Then you'll still be my secretary until I retire, and this girl takes over the business."

"This girl needs a name."

"We'll start a list, how about Mildred?"

Angie smacked his hand. "You don't get any more ideas if that was a serious suggestion."

Levi winked at her and then crawled forward and kissed her deep. "There is something I wanted to talk to you about that I realized at lunch you didn't know."

"Oh shit, what?" she asked and pushed him back.

"It's tradition for the male demon to take his wife's last name."

"You want to be a Walsh?"

"Nothing would make me happier," he assured her and then they were kissing again.

Angie was happier than she'd ever been. She was pregnant and she had a man who loved her so much it bordered on obsessive. She knew that she and her baby would never want for a thing in their lives. "I wish it hadn't taken us so long to get here," she mumbled against his lips.

"Maybe it had to be this way," he shrugged. "Maybe we never would have found each other without the goddess' help."

"And the witch's."

"Unfortunately," he grumbled.

"Don't worry, we don't have to invite Felicity to the wedding or anything, but I have to give credit where it's due."

"By that logic we might owe it all to the massive amount of alcohol you drank at your one-year anniversary party that led to you putting the appointment on my calendar."

Angie laughed. "I think you're right. Seriously though, I want it small and I want it after the baby comes so I can wear a dress I really like. I want to do it in Montana, outside somewhere in the summer."

"I think that will be perfect."

"And I don't want Foras to throw you a bachelor party with vampire strippers."

"Jealous?"

"Very," she snarled and he smiled at her as if it were the cutest thing he'd ever seen.

"I think you're forgetting that I am a demon and once a demon male has been chosen and committed himself to a female, there is no desire for anyone else."

"Are you committed?" she asked, feeling silly that she needed the reassurance, at least one more time.

"Until I die," he said, then set about proving it through multiple orgasms and a home cooked dinner.

The next day Angie dressed with particular care. She put on a simple purple dress that was loose enough still to fit and tight enough to show her belly, which seemed to be growing daily. And if she wasn't mistaken, she'd felt something move in there. She wasn't sure though so she hadn't said anything to Levi.

"Ready?" he asked as they rode down in the elevator.

"No, but we have to do it eventually."

As soon as they stepped out of the elevator Sharon's eyes locked onto the stone on Angie's finger.

"Thank the lord, or is this—well we need to talk," she said, sending Angie a meaningful look.

"I think this is the first time Sharon's been caught off guard," Levi whispered which earned him a scowl from the woman.

"How about lunch? Me, you, and Patrick," Angie told Sharon who nodded eagerly. "I'll send him a message."

"No worries, I'll grab him the next time he walks by. That boy is through this lobby a hundred times a day ever since that handsome fellow started working in marketing."

"Sam?"

Sharon nodded.

Angie was shocked. Sam wasn't the type that Patrick usually talked about. For one, he wasn't a supernatural of any kind, just a human. He was also average looking, but he was very kind too. The more she thought about it, she really liked the idea of her friend settling down with someone who was sweet and not so dangerous.

Patrick didn't wait until lunch, the rumors of Angie's ring flew through the office and he was standing at her desk less than an hour later.

"Tell me it's real!"

"Well, I'm sure it is, Levi isn't the type to buy fake jewelry," Angie said.

"No, I mean the proposal, the marriage, the whole in love with your boss who's also the father of your baby. Tell me it's real, a real life fairy tale."

Angie blushed and nodded. "It's real."

"You deserve this," he said emphatically before oohing and aahing over her ring.

At lunch she told Patrick and Sharon the whole story and they both assured her that they would fly to Montana for the wedding without hesitation. Angie teared up at that because she wasn't sure she'd ever had friends that would have done that for her. When she married Grayson they had done a small ceremony in town and half the people they invited didn't even bother to make the twenty-minute drive. She'd also not heard from any of them since the divorce and move.

"I'm so glad I found you two," she sniffled.

"Hormones," Sharon said, handing her a tissue while Patrick looked uncomfortable.

"Okay, now, tell me everything about Sam," Angie demanded, she needed a distraction.

Patrick blushed. "Well, I don't know, he's just so sweet and cute and he sends me messages every day telling me that he likes my shirt or that I did a good job with something. I started bringing him coffee and he asked me out."

"Like on a date, not a go to the vamp club and fuck, but a date with dinner and holding hands?" Angie asked.

"Yeah, he wants to take me to dinner and a movie this weekend."

"And—" Sharon prompted.

"And I said yes."

They all squealed in delight, gaining annoyed looks from customers around them in the sandwich shop.

Angie was feeling really good when she got back to work and went into Levi's office. He was sitting behind his desk, leaning back with his hands behind his head. He looked like a millionaire businessman playboy, which is exactly what she'd thought he was when she'd first come in for an interview. His eyes were closed but she knew he sensed her standing there in the doorway, his body had twitched and his mouth had lifted slightly.

"You just going to stare?" he asked, confirming her suspicion.

"The day I came in to interview for you I thought you were the most beautiful man I'd ever seen in my entire life."

He sat up and looked at her with a raised eyebrow.

"I thought there was no way you'd hire me and that if you did I'd spend every day with wet panties because you were a dream to look at."

"And did you?" he asked darkly.

"Mostly, yeah."

"What about on the days when I was an asshole?"

"Even some of those because when your voice gets low and growly," she trembled and stepped toward him, shutting the door behind her. "I want to feel that vibration on my core."

"Come and get it, baby," he said in that low way that drove her crazy. She locked the door and sauntered across the office. He leaned back slightly in his chair, his dark eyes locked on her the entire time, his hands still behind his head.

"Sir," she said in a high voice. "I really need this job, I'm sorry I took such a long lunch."

"I don't tolerate people taking advantage of me, Ms. Walsh."

Angie bit her lip to keep from smiling as she moved to the front of the desk and leaned forward with her hands on it. "Please, Sir, isn't there something I can do to make up for it?"

"I like my employees to be hands on when the clock is ticking and since you wasted some of that time, I think you'll have to work double time."

"I can work with both hands, Sir, let me show you." Angie walked around the desk.

Levi stayed leaned back, only shifting the chair to face her. Angie reached out and grasped his shoulders lightly then ran them down his chest to his belt. She locked eyes with him as she unbuckled his belt then slowly released his button and zipper. She could feel how hard he was and she wasn't lying about how often her panties were wet in his presence. Her hands shook slightly as she pulled his cock free of his pants and boxers. She did as promised, using both hands to run up and down his length a few times until he groaned. Then she pushed one hand further into his boxers and cupped his balls as the other continued to stroke his length.

"Oh fuck, Ms. Walsh, I can see that you really want to keep this job," he said, his voice gruff and shaky. His hips twitched but he still kept his hands up behind his head and Angie loved the power she had in that moment, despite the role they were playing. She felt as if he were at her mercy and she reveled in it. She knelt in front of him and took him deep in her mouth.

That was more than he could take apparently because she felt his hands in her hair. She sucked, stroked, and fondled him, knowing how he liked it.

"Good girl, take me deeper," he ordered darkly and lifted his hips, thrusting deeper into her throat until she felt tears prickle her eyes. She loved that feeling, loved when he took control of her and took what he wanted from her. It wasn't long before he growled and pulled her roughly away. She quickly found herself turned and pushed over the desk. He lifted her dress, moved her wet panties to the side, and thrust into her.

"Fuck you're so wet for me, baby. Did sucking my cock do this?"

"Looking at you behind your desk did this," she gasped as he thrust into her. One of his arms wrapped around to hold her slightly away from the desk, protecting her stomach even as he lost himself in her. He thrust over and over until she knew he was about to come. She could feel his trembling, his frantic thrusts.

"I need you to come, now baby, come for me," he pleaded and slipped his other hand between them to rub at her clit.

She didn't need any more than that. She buried her mouth against her arm to muffle the scream as she came around his cock and then he followed, burying his own screams in her hair and neck.

He pulled her with him down to his chair. She sat in his lap, his cock still buried in her.

"We've never done that here before," she said, breathless.

"Because I respect you too much to let anyone in this office hear your orgasm screams."

She laughed. "What about yours?"

"That too, it's awkward when you know what your boss sounds like when they come."

"I hope I can get over it," she teased.

"The best way to get over something is exposure therapy, so I guess we'll just have to keep doing this until you can look me in the eye in a meeting without hearing me panting your name."

She wiggled in his lap and his cock began to harden again. "Exposure therapy sounds like a good idea because I think every time I look at you I'm going to remember how your cock felt deep in my throat as you called me a good girl."

Levi grasped her hips and started to move her on his cock. "Touch yourself," he demanded.

Angie slipped a hand between her thighs and stroked her clit as he moved her up and down his cock. Their second orgasms were faster than expected, surprising them both with their intensity despite having just come. When they were sated and cleaned up, Levi pulled Angie in for a tight hug and a deep kiss.

"You are amazing."

"Thank you, Levi, you are pretty great too," she teased and walked out of his office feeling thoroughly fucked in the best way.

CHAPTER 29

There was one person that Levi wanted to personally inform of recent developments with Angelica. He made the arrangements and headed out in the afternoon. He sat at a coffee shop to wait.

"If you want to hire me to help with your stalking of a new girl, I might not take the job. I'm not sure I was doing what was best for Angie, and she's a sweet lady." Dalton sat next to Levi and waved the waitress over, ordering a large coffee to go.

"No, nothing like that. I wanted to tell you in person that it all worked out well. Angelica and I are engaged."

"No shit?"

"Yeah, I thought you'd like to know."

He looked doubtful. "Is this another one of those tricks? Some kind of trap you set and snared her further into? I know what you did getting her pregnant."

"If you were so worried, why haven't you come and tried to make sure she was okay?" Levi asked, annoyed that this young man thought he had any right to defend Angelica and at the same time, so glad that he did. Angelica deserved to have people looking out for her.

Dalton held up his phone. "We text. I actually already knew about the engagement. I was just bustin' your balls."

Levi liked that even less. "You shouldn't text another man's wife."

"Not married yet, but yeah, I get it. We're just friends and I asked for a weekly update so I'd know if she needed help getting out of the tower you stuck her in.

"Did she ever—" Levi stopped, he wasn't sure he wanted the answer to that question.

"Did she ever ask me to come save her? No man, she didn't. She insisted that she was fine and could handle whatever you were up to. She's a strong woman, I hope you're ready for that."

He was more than ready.

When Levi walked into the penthouse a little later than usual he was shocked by the smell of cooking.

"Oh hell no," he grumbled and walked to the kitchen.

Angelica was there. She'd changed into a pair of sweats and one of his T-shirts. It looked good on her and he wanted to slide his hands up under it where he knew he'd find her breasts uncovered. She complained constantly about wearing bras now, a side effect of the pregnancy he assumed. Maybe he'd take her shopping over the weekend to find something more comfortable. Now that they were engaged she couldn't complain about him spending money on her. In fact, he'd need to give her the credit card in her name that he'd gotten last week and keys to a car he had also purchased. When she'd taken Henley to the beach in hers he'd nearly had a panic attack, the thing was a death trap.

First, he needed to deal with this situation.

"What do you think you're doing?" he growled.

She jumped from the counter and turned, knife in one hand and a piece of raw chicken in the other.

"Jeez, why would you scare me like that, I could go into labor."

"Nope, too early to worry about that. Answer my question."

"I am cooking you dinner, I think it would be obvious."

"*I* cook *you* dinner."

"Yes, and I wanted to return the favor."

"No."

"No?"

"Just because I have gotten my ring on your finger, Angelica, that doesn't mean that I am going to stop caring for you in every way possible. That's not the way demons do things."

She relaxed and set the chicken and knife down, washing her hands. Then she walked to him and put her arms around him. She locked her caramel eyes on him and frowned. Levi didn't like that.

"I love you. I told you that, right?" she asked.

"Yes."

"And I agreed to marry you, like do the whole forever thing with you, right?"

"Yes."

"I don't want a life with you where you feel like you have to keep proving yourself to me."

Levi shook his head and wrapped his arms around her back. As he'd thought, he felt no bra under the thin cotton shirt and it made his cock instantly hard. "It's not like that, I don't feel like I have to prove myself to you anymore, it's more that I want to care for you. It's my love language." He'd heard the term before and hoped he was using it right.

Angelica lifted up on her toes and he bent down to meet her for a kiss. "My love language is physical touch, I hope you don't mind," she said as her hand slipped down to cup against his cock, making it harden even more.

"You know I don't," he whispered huskily against her lips then kissed down to her neck and nipped at her soft skin. "Why don't you go relax and I'll finish up in here, then later we'll see about that physical touch thing."

She sighed but obeyed, moving to the living room. "I can't even be mad, because you are a damn good cook."

"Lucky you."

"I am," she agreed and his heart swelled.

EPILOGUE

"I haven't had enough time," Angie groaned as another contraction ripped through her.

"I'm sorry, but the baby has," Dr. Brunswick assured her as she told her to push.

Levi was holding her hand and Henley was on her other side offering encouragement. Angie was about to push their daughter into the world after only six months and she didn't feel ready. They had the nursery done, all the diapers and blankets were purchased, she even had hired and trained a temporary replacement at work. "We didn't do the classes, we watched some videos. That's not the same thing," she insisted.

"We read books and watched *many* videos. You are ready," Levi insisted.

"What if I'm not good at this?" she cried.

Levi leaned down and kissed her forehead. "You are going to be an amazing mother because you have wanted it for so long."

"What if I don't like you when this is all over?"

Levi just smiled at her. "Well, we haven't gotten married yet so I guess it's still okay to change your mind."

She glared at him, that was not what he was supposed to say.

"Just relax, you're doing great, love," Levi assured her. "We'll deal with everything else once our daughter is in our arms. Now, push, let's meet our girl."

Angie bore down and put everything she had into it. Five pushes later there was a crying scream from tiny lungs and she was holding her girl.

"She's perfect, just like her mother," Levi said and kissed her forehead.

"What's her name?" Henley asked.

"Delilah Moon Walsh," Angie said and kissed her fiancé. She didn't love him any less in this moment, in fact, she thought she loved him even more.

"That's beautiful," Henley said. "I'll go tell grandma."

"She doesn't like being called that," Levi warned.

"Perfect," Henley said and walked out of the room.

"She looks like you," Levi said.

"How can you tell? She's just a bald sleeping mess right now."

"No, look closer."

Angie leaned closer to her daughter's head and grinned. There was the slightest fuzz and it was definitely more red than black. "Did you catch a look at her eyes?"

"No, she was squeezing them shut and screaming before she touched your chest and fell asleep."

"Are demons born with blue eyes like humans?"

"Nope, black from birth, so we'll see soon if she takes after me there."

"I think she has your skin tone. She's more olive than pale like me, I think that will look really good with the red hair."

Lamia pushed into the room then, despite the urging of a nurse who was cleaning things up. She nudged Levi out of the way and leaned over Angie. "Let me see."

"Say hello to your granddaughter," Angie said, moving the blanket away to show Lamia the entire tiny thing.

"Perfection, absolute perfection. Levi you did good chasing after this girl, and Angie, you made a perfect little baby."

"Thank the goddess," Levi said.

Angie whispered her own thanks to the goddess as she gazed at her daughter. There was no universe where she could be happier than this, and it was all because the Moon Goddess wanted to cause a little chaos.

MEET THE AUTHOR

Courtney Davis is an author of paranormal romance. She lives and teaches in North Idaho with her family and animals. She has always been interested in the possibilities of the supernatural and what it would be like to knowingly live beside them. Especially when there are relationships that cross species lines. She hopes that readers find an escape in her books just as she finds when writing them.

OTHER TITLES FROM 5 PRINCE PUBLISHING

Having the Demon's Baby *Courtney Davis*
Recipient *H.L. Voss*
Just Until the Wedding *Emi Hilton*
Having the Werewolf's Baby *Courtney Davis*
Courting the Lion *S.E. Reichert*
Mistress and Mage *Blythe Brandenburg*
Having the Vampire's Baby *Courtney Davis*
Come to the Cape *Emi Hilton*
Time To Byrne *S.E. Reichert*
Bookish *Bernadette Marie*
Dare You to Choose Truth *Lauren Lipp*
Enlightenment *Nicole James Kelley*
All the Little Moments *Savannah Reed*
The Rocking of the Ocean *Barbara Matteson*
New to Newport *Emi Hilton*
Trusting the Alpha *Courtney Davis*
Sweet Summertide *Sarah Dressler*
No Words After I Love You *S.E. Reichert*
Demons and Tea Leaves *Courtney Davis*
Shadow of the Throne *Russell Archey*

www.ingramcontent.com/pod-product-compliance
Lightning Source LLC
LaVergne TN
LVHW091044080826
845145LV00002B/619

* 9 7 8 1 6 3 1 1 2 4 4 0 2 *